Dedication

• • • • • • • • • • • • • • • • • • • •

I think I'll dedicate this to anyone who's ever felt like they've

had more to offer than what they were encouraged to give.

Chapter 1

2282—16

. . . .

"There's nothing wrong with helping people, even if there was, I shouldn't get in trouble for it," I muttered as I pulled my make-shift jacket tighter. *Oh really? Then why are you walking through the streets hiding your face when it's getting dark out?* My inner head voice slash conscience or whatever it was needed to stop talking. *Make me.* I sighed and forced my numb fingers to grip the light I had built from things laying around the house to illuminate the pitch black night. I stopped walking for a second to pick at my heel. I had been walking all day and I had noticed something different. There had been a Shipment earlier that morning,

Shipments were the government delivering the newest mandated clothing, voting tablets, and other equally exciting things. That morning it had been shoes, which were the exact same plastic that molded to the bottom of your foot and hardened that we'd always had, except now the plastic was a clouded white color and about 3 times heavier. My internal complaining came to a screeching halt when I heard a crash.

Don't move. Don't move, and they won't notice the only person outside, or the fact that you're holding a light that's as bright as the sun. I heard footsteps crunching on the edge of the plastic street where it abruptly ended and became roughly strewn gravel. I felt my heart pound as I started running. The footsteps behind me slowed and came to a stop. I forced myself to speed up, I heard a quiet click, and suddenly my feet wouldn't move.

I fell onto the hard plastic street with a thud. I ignored the throbbing waves of pain emanating from the bottom half of my body. I frantically looked down and saw the rigid, milky plastic straps that had been the source of my fall and the sharp pain in my ankle. No doubt they had been strategically placed to secure around my ankles so I wouldn't break anything. *So much for that.* I gritted my teeth.

Magnets. *I knew it.* I wanted to kick myself, but seeing that wasn't an option, I twisted my neck around to try and look at the heavy footsteps slowly approaching.

"Miss Finche, please accompany those two men to your house." A booming voice using an Amplifier said. They had turned off their light so I didn't see the owner of the voice, but I had a pretty good idea of who it was. I ignored my orders for a moment to glare at the road. *Magnets.* Magnets in the shoes, and in the piping and temperature controls under the street, I was disgusted I hadn't noticed earlier.

I turned around to see two large people walk over, the one on the left had a huge grin and the one the right looked slightly worried. My tensed shoulders lowered slightly. I sighed and tried to twist my arm to wave them over. I felt a sudden release then my ankles dropped from their crooked position. I looked at my feet which were numb and throbbing. *Hmm, must be remotely controlled.* I put my hands on the ground as I tried to get up, I slipped, and as I fell a shoulder suddenly materialized beneath my arm and helped me up.

"*Men*, not the word I'd use to describe you two," My voice caught and I quickly brought my hand to my throat, plastering on a rueful smile. I pushed off my helper and forced myself to swallow a moan as I forced my full weight on my feet.

"Me neither….Miss Finche," The one on the right mocked with a lopsided grin, oblivious to my pain. He was an outdated type of handsome. Dark hair and deep eyes. Rugged. That's the word.

The other one had light curls and brown eyes that seared into me, the one who I had pushed away. "I'm fine" I mouthed. I stopped myself from looking away and forced eye contact. I must've looked convincing. Unfortunately, I was a passable liar.

"Well, *I* do look the part" The one on the left pushed his brother lightly. I dug my twitching fingers into my elbows and rolled my eyes, trying to play along.

"Escort Miss. Finche, *Now!*" The voice was annoyed and cracked with irritation at the end.

I felt my heart beating rapidly. I looked over my shoulder, willing to accept the support I had denied before, but the siblings were too busy trying not to laugh at each other. I tried to force my irritation into a smile, straightened my shoulders, then started walking trying my best to put all the pressure on my right foot. *They should be taking this a little bit more seriously.*

"What were you doing tonight Miss Finche?" The owner of the voice; a man with a handsomely aging face asked. He had striking purple eyes that contrasted starkly against his black lips and pale blue skin.

His hair was composed of smooth black feathers that looked so soft I was really tempted to touch them. I knew I would look crazy petting an elected official's hair.

It would be even more awkward because my hand would touch his Real hair and not the feathers. Which in all likelyhood, was probably not that soft. It was also a pity that he was tapping his fingers impatiently on *my* dining room table. It's the unfortunate outcome of living in a world with no justice system. *He really needs to get on that.*

He cleared his throat. I looked at him and thought back to where I had been. The home of the two guys pretending like this whole thing was a joke. I had gone to the Medi district.

Medi's were people who worked their entire lives for Preps. Like the fake-o in front of me. Everyone hated Medis. Just because they weren't as smart—supposedly. The fake-o in question was leaning back haphazardly and his gaze was unfocused. A telltale sign that he was Trending, looking through any exciting news or scanning the latest fashion updates that only the ultra-elite got notice of the second they were released. It meant that I got time to rant internally, which wasn't really that different from any other day.

Even though Medi's grew and processed our food, fixed anything that we had that was broken, and all without complaint, they were still overlooked. And all because they were on the bottom of the three Tracks on the intelligence ladder.

Medi was the lowest rung of all of Society's population.Then came Prep, the Track I was unfortunately in, the average intelligence rung, then Accel. The smartest and holiest of all. It wasn't fair, but it wasn't going to change anytime soon (at least until I'm running the country). When you turn six, the Official

Educators test everyone and divide them into two different groups. if you don't test into the higher of the two, you're in Medi, then once the higher track tests, it splits into Accel and Prep. The different Tracks weren't really supposed to mingle, it was one of the many unwritten and unspoken rules of Society. So of course I had to break it. I gave Medis things that I had access to and they didn't. Which undoubtedly made me a good person. That alone put me in the "good human" section, where everyone else was not. By me giving away my abundance of stuff, it made me feel better about myself, and helped others, which was a prime example of a win-win situation. And it wasn't like the stuff I was giving away was any big deal. It wasn't important now, but when I was in charge and changing Society for the better, it would be the first step. Medis would have the same access everyone else did to tablets and other technology.

In 2050-ish, they invented a hard plastic that replaced glass, it couldn't be easily broken and was sensitive to touch. *Pretty much everything is made out of hard plastic, so boring.* They then made the internal wiring of old machines transparent. The tablets had wiring attached the to the plastic in between the screens and when you motioned a pattern in front of screen it turned on.

This technology was supposedly much more advanced than our predecessors' because it could project with bright colors and could be verbally or visually commanded. But the interesting part was inside. What we had was the rough equivalent to books. Since our planet was so dry and trees were all but nonexistent, books didn't make sense, they disintegrated, and could no longer be made. Not only did the lack of trees force us to use tablets, but it made us reliant on synthetic oxygen too.

Bummer number 1. Our technology was also limited because each tablet was dedicated to a certain topic or piece, again, like books.

Bummer number 2. If your hands get sweaty—which happens to *everyone*, you drop the tablets really easily and can break them. It's happened twice.

Bummer number 3. They're ridiculously expensive. Which meant that only rich people got access to information. Which is so messed up it hurts to think about for too long.

But the tablets in the old days could look up whatever the user wanted to know and could search this database of all this information and just learn whenever they wanted to. They had no idea how lucky they were.

We had to pay good money for anything that we wanted to learn that was outside of what they taught you in school. *Really* good money.

That's why all the kids in the Medi Track all ended up being civilian workers; they didn't have the qualifications to be anything more. So it was impossible to ever learn any more than what they're taught in school, since they didn't have the means to. That's where I came in.

I was the daughter of a Senator and a Director of Education. A Senator does....well, not much, and they earn tons, I can't really gripe about a Director, my mom seems pretty busy, but she also earns more money in a month than most Medis will in a year. Medis do so much and barely make enough credits to buy food and basic supplies. See—not fair. So I bought loads of old folk tale tablets and once I read them, I added on little things. I would take different materials from the moldable chairs around the house, I made containers and protectors for the tablets. And I took the wiring apart so there were no hard to understand hand motions to open them. Then I took them and gave them—

"Miss Finche!" My dad's boss—the feather haired dirt sack, was yelling. Apparently paying attention was only optional for him.

Should I sass? *No, you're not any good at it out loud.* The truth is brutal. So that would be my weapon of choice. *Nice metaphor.*

I looked him in the eyes. "I gave a little girl her birthday present." His blue face started turning a light shade of purple. *Daff would be so bent if she had heard that.* She could pass for a twelve year old, but if you pointed that out, you were in trouble. He squinted angrily. I thought he would implode; like '*generosity*, don't let it touch me, or I'll be contaminated.'

"Why?" He demanded.

I looked at him. *Really?* He cleared his throat as he realized how that sounded. Then he got angrier that I had made him uncomfortable. I tried not to smile, but not hard enough.

"Why were you in the Medi district?" He got a 3 out of 10 for trying to be professional.

"Because, a girl—in *Medi*, it was her birthday. So, I gave her a present." I crossed my arms and looked at him. "It's polite to give people gifts on their birthdays. At least that's what my mother tells me." I elaborated in case he had forgotten.

I remembered how excited Daff had looked. All for a little tablet on old stories. *Why was that wrong?* Was it wrong that I felt like I was needed? It wasn't wrong, it's just that he would never even think to go to a Medi's house. That would be unimaginable. Germs everywhere. So it would be hard trying to convince him that I treat Medi's like they're people. It wasn't wrong to help people. And he was majorly messed up if he thought it was.

"I understand that you might have felt obligated to—"

"But I wasn't obligated, Just like you weren't obligated to bring Q and L"

He shot me an irritated look. *That snark was for my ankle, you dirt sack.*

"The two…men, you had bring me, to my own house, yeah, they've got names." I looked over to the huddled figures whose shoulders shook with laughter. Q shot me a glance that said he was embarrassed of his name being known. If you couldn't tell by looking at them, their names gave away that they were Medis.

The ongoing Trend for baby names had been "exotic." Preps chose to keep sophistication on their side and use different animals and other stupid things as names. Medis never really got the memo. They also didn't use Profiles. And when they did, they were never up to date on Trends. They just did "favorites." Favorite letters, sounds, extinct things, and planets. I was surprised that I hadn't run into any foods yet. *"Oops sorry Tofu, didn't see you there."*

"Well," He said getting flustered. "You have to stop it." I tried not to imagine that the conversation was about a burly, bearded, upset man named Tofu. *Focus.*

I looked at him sharply, "Why would I stop?"

"It's not right Jessica. You're first in your class, you should be setting an example." He glanced over his shoulder, his feathers rustled when his head turned, *wow, designers are getting good*. "*Not by mingling with, them*." I rolled my eyes. I was only first academically, and it's not like it was a tough task to undertake. I needed a lot more to replace him one day, regrettably.

"Well no offense *Teak*, but I'm actually reaping all the rewards in these....*transactions*." He looked slightly relieved that I hadn't said anything that validated their being humans.

I continued, "Being the selfish person that I am," He looked taken aback, *he's relived you were the one to say it out loud*,"I *really* like feeling good about myself as a person, and I do that by giving the things that I know *I* don't deserve, to people who deserve it so much more than me. Then you know I love building things, so this is my building things in a very…non-destructive manner." I forced myself to look at him pleadingly, "I don't know why you would want to stop me from doing something *nice*—" *Oops*. Major misstep.

"Well, I'll tell you *exactly* what I'll do, *Miss Finche*." His thin ebony lips twisted viscously and his violet eyes shrunk to slits. *Uh oh, extra emphasis, I'm in trouble.*

"You're on probation." *What?* His smirk grew larger.

"If you fail to behave yourself as a Prep would—"

"Can you just explain what I've done, because I don't think it's wrong," I snapped. I glanced behind Teak and I saw L's face pale.

He breathed in sharply. "Well, you've, been, out! Out during curfew, and you've been destroying and *illegally* selling tablets!" *We don't even have laws. How can something be illegal, and why would you put emphasis on it?*

"But you can't—" He cut me off.

"Your probation period starts tomorrow. and if you fail to behave. There *will* be consequences." He tried his best to not sound pleased.

"What consequences?" His face turned a deep shade of mauve.

"You'll change to a different Track! Just being *smart* won't get you that far" He spat out. *Well, at least he followed through on his threat.* He quickly stood up and brushed off his jacket that trailed to the floor. He shot me one last withering glare before he strode out my front door. After I heard the sliding doors hiss as they shut and sanitized the air, I sighed and looked over, I saw Q and L walk closer. I remembered when I was admitted into Prep.

"So that's the President of Society huh?" Q asked offhandedly, looking at his reflection in my window. I nodded wearily.

"Well, with a country with a name as pretentious as 'Society,' you shouldn't expect any less." I quipped to hide my swirling thoughts. What did he mean switch Tracks? Tracks are for life, you can't just..switch. *If I switch I can't be President.*

"Well, it's a good thing he doesn't have to be liked by people anymore, otherwise he'd be—" He sliced his hand over his throat and made his neck go limp as he stuck out his tongue.

"It'll be different when I'm President." L stiffened after I spoke, but after and my questioning glance, his features softened.

L saw the look on my face and punched my arm lightly, "Hey, if it makes you feel any better, we can have you make him a scale and I'll take one of Q's mirrors, and we can drop them on his doorstep." I smiled at that. It probably took L a while to think of the fact that his Profile wouldn't hide his weight from a scale, or his real face from a mirror.

"If he makes me switch Tracks, let's do it," I said in all seriousness, unconsciously rubbing my ankle. *He won't do it. He can't.* "Like he could hide, we *literally* live in a bubble."Q quipped. I opened my mouth, but L beat me to it; "It's not an actual bubble, it's more like a dome-y thing, made of basically indestructible plastic that goes up for a mile or two. And there are vents

everywhere—"

"Thanks for the history lesson, but I think I'll pass." Q cut him

off disgustedly. That was pretty spot on. Not for the first time, I

wondered if L was in the wrong Track. I looked at L and really

noticed him, the way when he stood, his broad shoulders flexed

under his stained work outfit when he was getting irritated. *Woah,*

no! No looking at L. Creep.

"Hey pass me a water bottle, will you?" L looked worried and I

held my hand out impatiently.

I took it with a muttered thanks as I noticed his jaw

twitched. I never figured out how guys did that, the little jump in

the muscle of their cheek. I turned away quickly as I realized I had

been staring. *Again.*

I took the water bottle and put my thumb on the sensor.

It quickly scanned, measured heat then calculated that my

lukewarm thumb needed slightly cold water. I groaned. I pulled down my shirt sleeve and smushed the sensor against my armpit. I tried not to make eye contact as the bottle read my heat levels and sent the coolant to almost maximum so that it came close to forming ice. I felt a slight pinch from the drastic temperature drop and pulled my water bottle out from under my arm and brought it to my right ankle, making sure the sensor was facing up.

Q cleared his throat at my uncommon display of skin and tried to continue conversation. I huffed and pretended I wasn't embarrassed. "We could always find a way to turn off his Profile," Q said slyly, raising his eyebrows. I looked over at L who I hadn't noticed before, but never broke his gaze, I pretended to check the temperature on my bottle.

"I actually think that might genuinely kill him." I smirked.

"We can only hope," Added L, his warm eyes twinkling.

Chapter 2

. . . .

I tried to give myself a pep talk as I climbed the steps to Verde.

You *are* a good daughter. You *do* care about Trends. You *support*

your mom's pastimes. I was never a good liar when my mom was

involved. I was going to have to try really hard to keep all of my

thoughts *inside* my head since I was on *probation*. I had decided that

I would follow Teak's lead, and *firmly* believe there was *no such*

thing as *too much emphasis*. He became President *somehow*.

Verde was a local restaurant that my mother loved to host

parties at. February 26th, my birthday, was an excuse for my mother

to show off her money. I was turning sixteen and that was all the

encouragement my mom needed. My mom was kind of, off, but she

didn't start that way. When I was little, she had been the most

unique, exciting, amazing woman I had ever met. When I grew up, she became more involved in her work, which was great that she was passionate about it, but she got common. As it got worse, she'd want to frequent the social scene, then one day out of the blue, she started wearing her Profile. After I had worked up the courage to ask her why, she said in passing that it made her job easier. I figured my mom had officially gone common. Sometimes bits of her old self shined through the cracks of her Profile. But that meant that she had to be around long enough for it to show.

When I was younger we'd have these competitions of Who Can Number Better, *don't judge the title.* She always won, you'd start off with a number, square it, divide by three, add seventy-two or whatever, then whoever said the answer first won. She always won. She could multiply any number, not matter how big. My mom—the old her, was my hero, so in memory of that, I was going to play nice.

Plus, she didn't even know that the President himself had come to threaten me, at *our* house. She would've been thrilled to brag to her brood of puppies—I had read a few tablets from "The Dark Age," and they called followers puppies, *Don't know, don't care. I sound hip, so it stays.*

I waited for the wide sliding glass doors to hiss open and let out a gentle stream of air then for the several second long dusting of sanitizing air, I walked through and looked around for my mother. She was easy to spot. She was one of the tallest people around. My mom was slightly edgy in that sense. Tallness had never really been a Trend but she kept up with it. It had something to do with her never being tall since without her Profile, she was 168 cm tall. We measured.

I looked at her; hundreds of long spotted caramel feathers sloped over her forehead and gently spiraled near her chin. They were different from Teaks' and seemed to fit her better, the feathers looked, well, natural. Her skin was a dark luminous black that shined, and in the light looked blue. I remembered that she had been the one to explain to me what Profiles were.

She took one of my dolls, and grabbed a cloth. She had sat me down and made sure I was focused on the lesson. She would tap the base of my skull, where my currency chip was, and told me that was where Profiles were controlled too. She explained that everyone was basically hooked up to one big screen so they all saw the same thing. Then she pulled up my doll and told me it could walk around looking like a cloth if it wanted to, and everyone would see a cloth. But the kicker was that the doll was still there, you could still touch and feel it, you just didn't see it. I was having difficulty remembering her without her Profile as I looked at her.

I looked around the room and could tell by the pale aqua faces that surrounded her, she was going out with a bang. My mother gracefully stood up out of her chair. She lifted her chin, feathers

swaying softly, and waited for me to walk over. I felt the dozens of

eyes that followed me, it wasn't unusual for people to mistake me

for a Medi, but then they usually realized that my mom was

definitely NOT Medi, then they usually settled for haughtiness. I

could almost hear their thoughts.

Who is she? Why is she so plain? Is she trying to go Natural, she so

doesn't have the chin for it. What made her turn off her Profile?

I made sure not to walk near the mass of people were sitting. If I

got too close I knew that my Profile would make a pinging noise

that would start from the base of my skull, and if I was within a

couple meters of them, I'd be able to see their full name hovering

above their heads. I didn't really care who they were, but it was

installed in everyones chip so you can identify people even when

they change their Profiles every time there's a Trend update..and

they could afford it. The labeling was helpful if you couldn't remember names, and irritating if you were in a large group setting, it sounded like dozens of little explosions in your head. My mother always had a group of friends or acquaintances around. So many in fact that they had to put together two tables that each fit nine people. They were only temporary of course (both the tables and the people); they would never be heard of or mentioned again after tonight—the people that is. *But no one ever talks about furniture, so technically—*

My mother had taken it upon herself to meet as many wealthy and sought-after people she could. I had absolutely no idea why. Actually, I mean, it kind of made sense.

Everyone in Society, well Prep actually, had to run for their "position." You start qualifying during school by ranking high enough in your class. It's on the Leaderboard. It shows both popularity and academic rankings. Only the top 10 slots on both sections were of any importance. Most of the time, the top jobs were Government positions, which are the most sought after, but those who don't make it, get to be the Educators and other lesser-known evils, which is an absolutely awful system. All of my teachers were basically rejects. But not my mom, she had what it took to be first, whatever it was that they selected you off of in the educational careers. I was going to be first, play their stupid games, and end up in charge so I could change their weird rules.The rules that my mom helped make.

She's incredibly intelligent but I couldn't wrap my head around the fact that she wore her Profile like everyone else. But at the same time was so... opposite of the people she surrounded herself with. Kind of like those old lizards that changed colors to blend in, but that never actually affected the lizard, just it's appearance. *That thought took me way too much effort, looks like I've already been tainted by my surroundings.*

Mom made sure that all meeting places were lavish and expensive. And Verde was at the top of that list. I think it irritated her, that this was the only top tier restaurant, she loved variety. But she did love that they were *very* exclusive. You didn't just have to have money, you had to have *status*. I wondered if they would let me in if I wore a shirt that said ON PROBATION.

"*Jessssica,*" She made sure to draw out my name in a desperate attempt to flaunt and make it sound as beautiful as possible. But in reality it made her sound like a snake with a lisp. Mom had pushed the name, her moms' middle name. I thought it was a pretty half-hearted attempt on her side. At least give me her first name, don't make it....meh-ish. It was like she was telling me that she loved me, so she named me after her role model and inspiration, but she didn't love me *that* much. It wasn't exactly what my dad was aiming for either.

I found it ironic that he had wanted to give me a unique name, like Aphrodite or Tasmania. I had never met anyone else named Jess. So in a weird twisted way, my dad got the uniqueness that he strived for.

"Happy birthday." She said it as she raised the corner of her mouth, it looked like a smirk. I'm sure she meant well, but the Trend was to look like you're in a constant state of tragedy. Moving your face muscles was *so* out. Looking like a corpse was *so* in.

She sat down on her chair and motioned for me to do the same with a flick of her wrist. Apparently regality was also a passing fad. As soon as I sat down, a suck-up turned to me and gave a wide fake smile. I kept my face impassive, this normally didn't happen, people wanting to get to my mom through me. *Ugh.*

"So, what's it like? The big one-six?" His voice was lilting on the consonants and sharp on the vowels. I studied his face, his skin was a pale shade of aqua, definitely out of style. I could tell he was desperate to elevate his social status, and like many other people, for some reason thought that if they were nice to me, my mom would automatically make them worthy of her friendship.

"It's kind of like being fifteen, but it feels like, I don't know what, but *something*, has been added to my life." His eyes were blank but he nodded sagely. He suddenly smiled brightly—a big no no, as my mom stood up. She looked around and turned to speak to the amassed group of people chattering away, not paying attention to the pathetic mass of human labeled ATLANTIC P. I had taken her attention for long enough, she was focused on better things. Like glaring at my father's boss's secretary who didn't technically-but-almost-sorta came without an invitation, he glanced at her briefly, and didn't try to hide a snicker.

I wearily glanced over my mothers' brood; I saw colorful, thin, beautiful people. I didn't like any of them. I would've much rather been talking to Q and L. Even better, Daff.

I looked down at the table I saw the scratched edges in the smooth white table top. I saw scrapes on the edge of the automatic chair sliding system from where all of these people in disguises had roughly pushed their seats in effort to slide out quickly, after they had decided the retraction path was on too slow a setting. Even in a seemingly perfect place with perfect people, there were still flaws. If I had pointed that out to mom she probably would've frowned, and been outcast from the land of fake, faker, and fakest for showing emotion. I was really tempted to bring up my meeting last night. I wanted to see her reaction. To see if she would care enough to break a Trend. I decided not to, so I could believe that she'd get upset.

I lifted my eyes from the floor to once again see the multitude of colors, feathers, and shiny things that all of these "in-style" people had drowned themselves in. I was wistful just for a second, imagining a malfunction at Head Quarters that would caused a sudden drop of Profiles.

People that had a second ago searched each other for any visible flaws, and who whispered secrets that were so cruel they seemingly took form, would now look for the nearest thing to hide them. If their looks weren't everything, then what did these kinds of people really have to live for? They would probably need a lot of therapy after the harsh realization they would be forced to face; that their entire existence was based off of a lie.

You're really messed up, you know? I ignored my conscience and focused on the table. Let's count the scratches. For the billionth time. It only distracted me for about a minute. I actually remembered that on this particular table, there were five weirdly long scratches. I could never figure out what made the shallow but lengthy gouges in the hard plastic. I hadn't realized I was stroking the table until the waiter came around and glared at me. Obviously he didn't get the Trend update, let alone the memo on customer service.

He was a perfect match to the little man on the menu left untouched next to my chopsticks. He had a stick thin body, paired with a mustache that curved delicately at the ends. I decided to forgive him for the glare—if only because he had beautiful facial hair. The twirls were drooping since I had upset the masterpiece.

One thing I liked about this restaurant was how they had all their servers change their Profiles while serving customers. All the men had a classic chocolate brown slicked back hair-do. All the women had pretty blue eyes and beige hair pulled back into severe, high pony-tails.

They started with my mother who held up her menu, her dark face shining, stoic as could be. I wanted to see what would happen if someone threw their dinner at her face. She's so focused on being fabulous that she probably would've just flicked it off and dabbed at her face. Maybe if it was in her hair I'd get to see a lip quiver. *You are a horrible, awful daughter.* I tried to keep a straight face. It was hard. I watched as she deftly pointed to something that was probably died green.

At any restaurant, all the food was the same. Sure, the flavors could be different, but they were all made of the same tofu like thing. A few decades ago they found a food substitute that had all of the necessary food groups that was based off of condensed seaweed, artificial proteins, and give or take a few preservatives. At all diners they had the same square mush, but at places like Verde, they spruced things up.

There are different flavors that they can inject, shove, or drizzle on or in the otherwise bland condensed slop. Not only did they have the basic Sweet, Sour, and Salty flavors, but at Verde they had something that was very unusual.

Verde used Profiles not only for their servers, but for the food as well.

They had figured out a way to attach Profiles to the bottom of their plates. They would make Profiles that showed elaborate architecture instead of mush. The servers would come around the corner bringing artfully woven bridges that looked incredibly intricate, with thin braided tofu strands swinging.

For the first few weeks that I first came to Verde, I would always order the specialty dishes. I would wait anxiously for my food and salivate at just the idea of how delicious it looked and would consequently taste, then when I took a bite, I wanted to gag. It was the same old tofu; it tasted worse because I had been expecting something so much better. It was probably Teaks' idea, just to torture me. So I rebelled by continuing to eat my ultra-appetizing sponge. Sometimes, if I wherein an exceedingly good mood, I would groan each time I took a bite out of my plain square tofu, just to make my moms' audience uncomfortable. They would start to doubt their culinary masterpieces.

Even though the edible art seemed like a great idea, there were still limitations with plate Profiles.

Each plate could only appear to be one specific dish. There really wasn't a difference between the food that was on those plates and everyone else's. The only difference was what you saw. And to these people, that made it all the better. I had figured all of this out by being my usual dazzling self and irritating the waiters. It was one of the best ways to dine. I would order then say, "Oh, but I want it to change to, um, this four story tower," I would say as I pointed to one of the most expensive dishes, "a quarter of the way through then change to a dull fuchsia instead chartreuse, then three eighths of the way, um, this one *must* be mauve," The waiters just sighed and one of the friskier ones developed an eye twitch, I was only semi-sure it was a glitch in his Profile. Then I would come back asking for different Profiles they didn't have, or for the food to be taller, or shorter, then move. I think it must have been the fractions that frustrated them.

If I had made the Profiles, the buildings would move, why couldn't they? They could program them to be practically anything, so why not have them move, or rain down dressings or flavors. They could be animals. From the before-Profile times, there were all these different flavors. Honestly, three flavors is a travesty. I had tried ordering all three an making different combinations, but all it does is make you slightly nauseous. A grade-A let down.

I waited until all the haughty guests had ordered, and then I pointed to the plainest order of tofu. The waiter raised his already disapproving-chocolate-brown eyebrows and said nothing. He wasn't the eye twitch one. I pretended I didn't notice. But I internally deducted points. No doubt, every member of my mothers' troop had ordered the most expensive plates with their own Profiles. Well good for them. I hoped the plates were ridiculously heavy and he fell over carrying them.

After I had endured two hours in the company of some of the shallowest people I had access to, we finally left. In a way I had enjoyed the dinner. I didn't have to say a word, and whenever I was about to I had been cut off. I had been ignored, silently ridiculed, and judged, but I didn't have to face the deathly silence of the house.

At the house, my mom looked at me, "Have a good birthday honey!" As I opened my mouth to tell her about my probation, she hugged me. I had reached too high up, I'd forgotten her Real height, and I stood hugging my mothers shoulders, where feathers should have been tickling my forehead, there was open space and I felt her Real curls scratch against my shirt. I hated hugging her with her Profile on, it felt like hugging someone with your eyes closed, but times three. I stepped back, she smiled and opened her mouth to say something and stopped, I saw her eyes drift above my head. She must've been reading about a new Trend that had just been released. She set her jaw like the programmers were out of their minds. Nonetheless she rushed to her wing of the house without a word, set on buying all the newest looks.

I looked around; dad wasn't home yet—shocker. I decided to duck into my room, grab my notebook, and explore.

Screw the probation. I was bored.

Chapter 3

. . . .

I walked out of the house, slung an Oxy-Pack over my shoulder, and rushed to the end of our neighborhood, only thirty houses away. When I had first gotten a notebook, it was one of the first things I wrote down, that and several poorly sketched graphs. Apart from that, I liked to keep things accurate and precise; I had decided there was no room for mistakes in my notebook. It wasn't like it was inside my head. I had endless notebooks. *Brain-books?* I wouldn't have been able to function without it.

I had hated my notebook at first.

After another unremarkable day, I was walking home from Medi after visiting Daff, and I saw it. There was this small stack tucked in the middle of a plastic crate by the side of the arched entrance to Medi. I had looked around the pristine milky road and scanned the empty street.

After one last search for people, I calmly sprinted over and started rummaging through it. There were around 10 short rectangular thin sheets. I had dragged by thumb across the edge and felt a sharp sting, I quickly shoved my finger into my mouth.

I had just cut myself with an unidentified object on the side of a Medi street. It was probably garbage or something toxic that was packed into delicate white sheets. I set my jaw and yelped as I bit down on my finger, and pulled out my thumb. I started going through lists of deadly toxins that could be flattened as I groaned and dragged it back to L. He had impatiently given me the sanitizing spray after I had insisted. I didn't tell him about the sheets, and he got irritated when I wouldn't tell him how I had gotten cut. I had yelled at him, then went home with my crate which I hid under his table and had retrieved after a speedy exit. A week later there had been another crate, but the time after that, it was bound and labeled PAPER. I bought all the tablets I could find that were about paper and finally ended up showing L after I had about fifteen paper facts on hand which were used to startle, silence, and impress. He had lifted one corner of his mouth, and his eyes would look into mine for a second too long, the way he did when he found something funny. Then we worked on using the Seamer to bind the pages together after a few prototype covers ended up in the trash. As he helped by giving moral support and a few tips on binding, I looked around their house. I thought of how L, Q, and Daff were happy. Despite not having amazing careers, a lot of money, or a big home. I compared his tiny house and large family to the huge homes with very few occupants of Prep. The other major difference was the happiness levels of the two settings.

Medi scored higher on that scale every time.

———————

I looked at all the Prep houses. Grand. Extravagant. Dull. All those words could have been used describe the identical homes that were no more than one story high. They all sat on massive plots of land and stretched themselves as wide as could be.

I had learned that in the in the Green Age and even before, they stacked buildings on top of one another. I wish they had done that with these. They were just so *boring*. Every. Single. House. *Ohh I wonder what color the house down the street is,* oh wait. It's creamy, disgusting, white, just like everything else in Society. It's supposed to be very clean, safe, and sterile. It's actually very gross, gaudy, and unoriginal.

If I were the Master Architect or whoever it was that designed the homes, I would've at least had some fun. No bridges between wings? No upper and lower levels? No hidden rooms with bunkers, and pass-codes, or secret knocks? No. Because no one on the planet had a shred of creativity.

I walked toward the end of the thirty house mark. This was where I turned stopped, hesitated and turned around. Or, at least I usually did. Ten more imaginary houses away was the clear, steep curved slope of what kept us safe and secure inside Society. I'd always thought about going outside the dome, but before I could think about going outside, there was one last barrier before the dome door.

A low—you guessed it; *white* fence sagged on the lip of the road. It was a curved street that never seemed to end; the low fence was the only way for Kilometers to cross the patch of rocks that was about a meter wide. Sad truth; it probably prevented any and all Preps from wanting to cross it. The risk of a twisted ankle would *not* be worth "exploration." Minus me of course.

There were rocks that I wasn't familiar with. I didn't really like that. I said that I hated Society people, but really I almost liked them. I liked them because there were never any surprises. I liked things being predictable, but different. I didn't want everyone to be the same, but I didn't want them to be, totally, volatile and surprising. That would be kind of awful. *Surprise! I bought you a blank plate Profile so you can hide things on the plate and no one knows that they're there!* I could imagine my mom doing something like that, then she would eat something invisible while everyone stared in shock, she would crack up. I bit my lip and my forehead creased. *That's not important, you have a decision to make.*

"If I walk to the building, I can come right back," I whispered, negotiating with my inner self, drawing myself back to the task at hand. No one would even know. Just me.

I took in a deep breath and slowly let it out. I saw the tall building that I always tried not to see, only a couple kilometers outside the dome. I had been walking home when I noticed it, I ran to the thirty house mark, and I saw it. The building had a Profile, It was flickering. The tall, sparkling white building had flashed and turned into a disintegrated crumbling two-story. I had gone back the next day, but someone had debugged it. It was back to the glimmering building of old. I didn't have the courage or supplies needed to make the trip, so this was my prepared state. I had been ready to explore, I brought Oxy-Pack; my synthetic oxygen pack—in case I ever went running or something as equally crazy, L had given me one he said he didn't need. I'd never thought that I would use it—*there's a very large possibility that it could be broken.* I was also on probation, and no matter how much I liked Medis, I didn't know if I would fit in there anymore than I did in Prep.

I tried to weigh in the consequences. I really did, but they just kept floating off the decision scale. I just wanted to *do.* Be all actiony. Unpredictable.

Pfft. This had gone on long enough. I lifted up my foot, clutched my notebook, and took a step. The stones crunched under my foot. *Progress tastes like victory. Sweet, and… progressive.*

I had never been this far away from home before. *Well technically Medi is further away when you think about it…* Well, as far as I had ever gone on *this* side of my house, I wanted to find a new place, and this was exciting, the most exciting thing I had done in a while. *Oh great, yeah keep doing dangerous things because they're enjoyable. No no, that sounds like a great plan.* I slapped my conscience. So hard that it shut up. This feeling was different than the one I had when I was giving tablets to Daff. It felt, bigger, more important.

I took one more wobbly step on top of the tiny rocks, and brought my leg up and—*thunk.*

My shin rammed into the old first generation construction plastic, I slid along the top of the fence, and sat there cradling my injured shin with one hand. My eyes watered. "Owww." *Shake it off.*

I stood up and repositioned my notebook in my hand, as I did that, I forgot to keep a hand on the fence and smacked down on the rocks I had been nervous about earlier.

I felt that I had suppressed my curiosity as I sat pathetically on the same side of the fence that I had always been on. I wanted to yell. Like really, really loud. I knew I was frustrated, then again I was always frustrated, but I had never really felt hate until that moment. And the victim of my emotional onslaught was none other than a rock, I was projecting. After I had read a Psychology tablet, I knew that everything I was blaming on the stone was directed towards none other than my fabulously graceful self. I was mad that this was a big deal, upset that this was something exciting. Angry I hadn't ever done it before, and disappointment that I couldn't even do *this*. I sat there and felt the pain rush up and down my legs.

I sighed; I knew it would hurt worse to get up. I let out a deep groan and lowered myself on the rocks and looked up.

From that angle, the rocks weren't as daunting, but the plastic dome made me feel, restricted—more so than usual. I watched the hazy sky and it looked like it was moving. I sat up, I let out a whimper as pain shot through the top of my thigh to my lower back.

As I was looking up at the swirling mass of grey, I focused my eyes on the tendrils of pollution that twisted around the dense layer above the lighter clouds. I took out my notebook and wrote: The sky moves. *You sound so stupid.* I had to save space so shortening was necessary. I remembered that we were actually on an enormous spinning rock, and that one of the most overlooked things was our sky, even though the sky, separated by several meters of the toughest plastic we could make, was always looking over us, we hardly looked up at it because it's always been considered ugly. And ugly things didn't really have a place in Society.

I remembered learning that, a century or so ago they used to have a blue sky since molecules in the air scatter blue light from the sun more than they scatter red light or something like that. Which didn't really even make sense to me, but I memorized a basic explanation to pull out whenever I needed it. Anyway, our notarially depressing grey sky was thanks to our forefathers who decided that they really didn't care how they left the planet for their children.

I wished we had a blue sky. Then we would be able to see the Outer Space at night. We wouldn't have all those gloomy clouds. It might've been even more depressing to look up and see pitch black, but would be nice to see that there were more places out there other than this dying planet.

I thought about it for a while more, I realized my thoughts were turning sour. I was going to play the Pretend game, since I was in the mood. Take all of the things I had to pretend didn't irritate me, and let them out. My mom made it up when I was little and Profiles used to scare me. She'd say, "Let's pretend they're like big toys, they don't think, you just have fun and play with them," Looking back on it now, my mom kind of helped me be more messed up than I originally was.

I hadn't played it in a while, and I was going to make myself feel better, like I have a pathetic life and thankyouverymuch for realizing it.

I started out whispering, "Let's pretend that ," My voice carried away in the open space and I finished the thought inside my head; Let's pretend that…I had a dad that told me how much he loved me and came home every night. Scratch that, actually showed up at the house. I could've pretended that I had a mom that was 100%

into my life and cared about me more than her job (and that she gave me a name that was all my own, not like a bad copy of someone else). I could've pretended I had a best friend who deserved the title; friend. I could've pretended I wasn't laying on a pile of rocks playing the stupid Let's Pretend game.

I realized I liked this feeling. Not the game, the game had actually left me feeling worse than I had originally started out.

I liked being away from everything Fake.

Here, at approximately 30 ½ houses away, I felt free. Free from the feather hair, the diamond eyes, and the boredom. The raw boredom of being able to guess *exactly* what the newest "problem" or "issue" was. I lied, I said I didn't like being unpredictable, but that's only because I was afraid of it. I didn't know it, and that's the scary part.

Just go to the building, it's like an embodiment of all your fears. It's the perfect metaphor. It'll be a turning point, of growth and stuff like that.

I unsteadily lifted myself up and turned away from the building. I didn't need to know— and my depressed mindset was telling me that my fears, dirt, and grime, along with everything else inside the building would kind of make me malfunction. I would be in emotional overload.

It didn't matter how far away I got, my mom would still be out spending her time with people, things, and looks that would always be Fake. I'd still be using my parents money to "help" people by rewiring tablets. I didn't know if I was even making a difference. My dad would still be at his office plastering pictures of his Fake face on everything not even attempting to be a mediocre parent like mom. Tal would still be the only friend I had in Prep. There would still be people that care about nothing but their looks. I would still be the only person who actually wanted anything to change. What did it matter how far I got? It would never be far enough.

Depressing was an understatement. What make it 100,000,000 times worse was that it was true.

Chapter 4

· · · · · · · · · · ·

I walked into my bland, boring house and stopped. I wondered if there had been toxins on the stones, because obviously I wasn't seeing clearly.

My dad was home.

He was stooped over. *Perfect time to attack. He's unsuspecting.* His back was turned away from me, but I knew what I would see if he turned around. His face stylishly aging—Fake. Jet black feathers that flowed into a soft grey fluff—Fake. Emerald green eyes—Real, I just wished the rest of him matched. I felt like interrogating him and asking why he worked for the Cesar of Society. *But admit it… Punching is calling to you just a bit more….*

Around his eyes was mostly smooth skin that harshly contradicted his ancient eyes. He looked haggard and hard, impenetrable.

"Hi Dad," I cleared my throat and took another step forward. If I tried hard enough, I could probably make him care about me. Or run away.

If he doesn't apologize, hit his throat with the side of your hand. He will *be sorry.* His eyes looked me over then hardened.

He's so getting a mouthful of fist. I winced, *that was such a bad insult.* I realized how I must have looked, disheveled and twitching; like a crazy person. As per usual.

I took another shaky step forward, "How was work? It was mom's birthday, and you weren't there..." He straightened from his slightly hunched position. *Did your boss tell you that he came to our house and threatened me, was it your idea?* I forced another step until I knew I would only have to take five more to be right in front of him. He still stood there, not saying anything. He looked me over once, disappointed.

"This whole Medi business needs to stop," *It speaks.* His voice was smooth and clear.

"Why?" I blurted as he walked past me.

The door shut behind him, I smiled as I felt warmth trickling down my face. *Don't cry. Go, and....hit him or something. Maybe a very light kick to the knee.*

"Shut up Jess," I hiccuped out, I groaned, I hated crying. I slid down the nearest wall and slammed my already bruised tailbone against the cold floor. I was more frustrated with myself for being all emotional than anything else. I roughly pulled my knees to my chest as I tried to control my shoulders shaking.

"You should've punched him," I shook my head and waited until I had sufficiently calmed down then wiped my eyes. I glared at my fist for lacking sufficient pain-inflicting capabilities. I winced as I tried to pull myself up, then gave up, and sat back down.

I must have fallen asleep because I remember waking up feeling my raw, tear stained face, thrown across my arms. I got up to shake blood into my hands as I walked into my room, trying not to run into the doors that scrambled to open before I hit them, while flailing my arms. I took off my shoes and let my feet fall on a rug-thing I had made out of old stained clothes, it was actually pretty hideous, it was a good thing it was on the floor. One of my very first prototypes. I stood for a second after I heard the resonating thud of my heels on the floor. I felt the corners of my mouth lifting. I lifted up a leg then dropped it. I did it again, and again, and again. I felt a smile trying to shove its way on my face until I heard my mom opening a door. I stood still for a moment until I shrugged my shoulders and stomped harder and louder. *You're going to get shin splints.* I heard footsteps approaching quickly. The smile I had tried to hold back was on full force, and I couldn't dim it, even if I tried. My mom opened the door and all of her regality

was gone. Along with her Profile. I hadn't seen her without it in a

while. She had light curls that I had always wanted and stormy

grey eyes that crinkled when she smiled, which lately, hadn't

happened that often.

"What in the world?" She asked as she looked at me.

"I'm trying to break the walls that restrict me,"

"Literally," We finished at the same time.

"Nice metaphor," She nodded approvingly. She was back in

Real-Mom mode, *finally.* I grinned so big that my bottom teeth were

fully exposed. It looked more like a creepy grimace than anything

else. She hugged me, and I let out a deep breath. Weird fact #456,

moms smell better than anything else in the world, the closest

description it is of colors and feelings. Which are not very good

descriptions at all. But to give an accurate description, my mom smelled like warmth and a deep brownish red. She held me for a good five seconds, a grade-A hug, before pulling away.

She looked at me, her eyes laser focused. "What's one hundred-forty times two-thousand fourteen, plus seven, minus twelve."

"This game's so unfair, you probably work on the problems, then know the answers—"

She grinned, "Ten seconds!" I sighed, "Umm, ok so two hundred-eighty one-thousand nine-hundred-sixty, plus wait, what do I add by?"

She shook her head and her curls bounced, "Five,"

"Mom! Not fair if I can't remember the numbers—"

"Three."

"You can't be serious! No, you're disqualified, that's garbage, trash actually, no way is that fair—"

"The correct answer was two-hundred eighty-one thousand, nine-hundred fifty-five."

I gazed at her cooly. "What's three cubed, multiplied by fourteen, divided by two, add one-hundred, square rooted?" I crossed my arms and smirked.

Her grin got wider, "Seventeen."

I glared at her, and grabbed my notebook from where I had shoved it in my pocket. I grabbed my pen and sat down at the bench near the counter. "What did I ask?" I mumbled.

"You said: 'What's three cubed, multiplied by fourteen, divided by two add one-hundred, square rooted,'" I wrote it all down, "three-hundred seventy-eight, two-hundred eighty-nine, seventeen," I glared at the paper. I never got to win that game.

"Thanks for making it such a pretty problem, didn't think it was going to turn out." She ruffled my hair then turned around and strolled to the kitchen. I followed and watched as she reached in the

Chiller. She pulled out a tofu square from the tower of neatly stacked blocks. She offered me one and I shook my head.

"Why are you so good at that?" I leaned back against the counter that was momentarily raised, I hated it when it was up, as soon as she left I would press a few buttons and make it slide back under the floor. She didn't seem to care about my internal plotting as she delicately pulled apart the block then ate the pieces. When I ate squares I just bit into them, but as I watched her it made me feel less-than regarding my eating habits.

"You're right there," She pushed her index and thumb together, "You've got the brain for it now it's just how you solve the problem. You can do the math, but you wait until you get the full problem before you solve it. You have to find a way to do it as it's being given to you. Be proactive, expect the next step and solve along the way, that way, by the end of the problem, you already have the answer."

"That was deep *ma mére*," I smirked. She rolled her eyes and gingerly chewed the tofu bars.

My mom had never finished the french Tablet that she had bought a while back and I loved rubbing it in. I didn't know why, but she pretended to know french and would out do anyone who thought they could do the same, I couldn't wait until she was discovered.

She'll start conjugating adjectives—which isn't even a thing that you do, and fling them into your face, she really tried to embody the phrase "fake it until you make it." What was so weird was that she didn't pick up languages like she did with numbers. So of course I make fun of that every chance that I got.

I saw her arm monitor blinking and I looked away as she tapped her wrist to answer. A second later, Fake mom was back and in costume. She had turned her Profile on and was walking out of my room.

"Bye mom," I reminded her I was there.

"Bye honey!" She managed to get out before she was pulled back to whatever new development had come up in the glorious and exciting world of Education. Well, I had her for a couple minutes. That's really all I needed.

Being angry took too much energy. Being sad was exhausting. So I took off my jacket and walked towards my silver sleep pod. As I was walking I remembered something odd. My mom didn't say anything about the notebook. I put it as a low priority and focused on my main mission; sleep.

I pushed two milky buttons on the side panel and waited for the quick release of air that signaled it was ready. I lightly lifted the plastic shells open. I pulled back the covers and gingerly sat until I could slide down enough to be able to sleep. I clicked the door button on the inside and the clear shells slowly descended over me. I was asleep before I heard the click that indicated it was sealed, I didn't even stir when it started seeping oxygen into my pod. I needed all my strength for what came next. I had a very long, boring day ahead of me. I had school.

Chapter 5

. . . .

I woke up to red haze coming through my window. I
angled my neck on my head rest so I could see across my bed. I was
thinking about what it meant, being in Prep. It meant I could make
changes, for the better. Tracks are supposed to be where you
belong, for life; the IQ tests make sure that you're in an
environment where your abilities will thrive. I didn't exactly feel
like I was thriving. Sometimes I wondered if I was really supposed
to be in Prep. I had taken the test with my best friend Tal. We had
walked through the doors and sat down at our desks giving each
other nervous smiles. I remembered our conversation before we
walked through the doors.

"We'll both be in the same group, right?" I had been anxious to hear her answer. "Of course!" She looked at me like I was crazy. Classic reaction after a Jess encounter.

"Let's be in Prep, kay?" She waited, "Just remember to answer all the questions like a Prep would and we'll be in the same class forever!" I quickly nodded my head and followed behind. The seats were the regular blue, uncomfortable, plastic ones that were in any classroom. It was the test area that was new.

It was like the wall came out at the sides so you couldn't see anything past it. Almost like a room with just three walls. When I sat down, a layer of plastic I hadn't seen before came out of the sides and closed around me so that there was no way I could get out. My breathing sped up as I tapped the plastic. I tried to pry my nail in the crack where the plastic had joined, but my nail was too thick to fit in the small groove. I swallowed nervously, turned around and sat in the chair. "It's all good," I murmured, I just had to finish the test and they'd let me out.

Since I couldn't anything else, it forced my attention to the screen that had big letters that spelled out my name. There were big white square letters on a headache inducing blue background. They then had six blocks that sat on the desk, on one side they were all white but had other sides that were either entirely or partially red.

I took a shaky breath. "What would a Prep do?" I whispered over and over again.

I jumped when the automated voice blasted out of the speakers. It asked me what my name was then the test began. On the screen it would show me a design that I had to make with the blocks. There was a tiny camera that was on the bottom of the monitor so it could scan a blue light and see if it was correct or not. After I completed the first three designs I could tell they were getting harder. I smiled, this was more fun than I thought it would be, Tal would—I had forgotten about Tal. I felt my smile drop. I remembered my promise.

I had to be a Prep. I knew that a Prep would take longer, but not too long to finish the designs. I forced myself to slow down and would flip the blocks a few times before I made each move. At last that portion of the test was finished and I felt like I had done exactly what a Prep would do.

I just wasn't so sure that I wanted to be a Prep anymore.

After that the screen asked me weird questions like; "How are a dream and reality related?" I was stumped on that one. I thought about it and finally said, "You want to change both of them, but that doesn't always happen." I didn't know if that was a very Prepared answer.

Then the screen asked me math questions and writing questions that popped up on the screen. Then I had to repeat the numbers that it said back, but in order. "five, seven, forty-three, two, ten, seventeen, and forty-five."

I didn't have to pretend for this one. "Two, umm, five, then uh, seven, ten, forty-five," I was nervous, what if I got into Medi?

What if I had taken too long with the blocks? I got even more nervous when they added letters.

"Now, JESSICA FINCHE, please repeat all the letters and numbers but put them in order, alphabetically, then chronologically, begin." The choppy generated voice asked me.

That was the hardest part. I remembered trying to scratch the letters and numbers on my arm but I couldn't remember them all and I couldn't read the scratches. The rest of the test I was sniffing back tears because I scratched a 4 in too deep.

The very last question was the trickiest. "JESSICA FINCHE," the voice said, "If something is broken, what do you do? A: Fix it, B: Leave it, or C: Make something better. You have thirty seconds."

I opened my mouth, C. 28. I wanted to say C, but I closed my mouth. 22. C wasn't a Prep answer. 17. I wanted to be with Tal, didn't I? I saw ten seconds left on the screen.

"B: Leave it" I answered. Accel didn't have Tal.

From this angle my eyes were unfocused and made everything blurry. I tried to distract myself from the topic my mind kept drifting back to; did I really hold anything back on the tests? They were designed to put you where you belonged. I was in Prep, for a reason, I might not have had what it takes to be in Accel, let alone Prep. *Ok, light uplifting airy thoughts, list your surroundings.* I couldn't see the seams of where my pod was sealed, but I saw all the dust lazily floating in the air and landing on top of the clear plastic.

Sometimes I wished that our world wasn't polluted by the people before us. My mind obviously didn't understand the term "uplifting." I wished that they had cared about us enough to protect and take care of the world that we lived in. But that was a tall order. If someone told me that when I fell on the rocks yesterday, those rocks would've been the only available building material for the homes of my great-great-great-great-great grandchildren, but I had ruined the pattern so the formations or whatever was all off, I would've said, well, looks like they're out of luck. So I couldn't *really* blame them. But I did it anyway.

I learned that back in the day, everyone would have their own vehicle and use it for traveling thousands of kilometers all around the world. They fed their hideous metal heaps oil. That's why our sunshine is red. The pollution did something to the outside layer of our planet. Which kind of made sense, like the earth had an even bigger dome that got clogged up with all of this....gunk.

The metal junk called, Forms of Transportation, such as Vehicles; would drive on roads, in skies, and in the oceans. They would feed them thousands of liters of petrol and they would spit out enormous amounts of hot air that helped warm up our planet. Another reason we had sleeping pods and a lack of good food.

Supposedly, there used to be a lot of land on earth. And there used to be ice caps, and seven continents. There used to be so much more, I remembered reading a few history tablets that had old maps, back then, only 2/3 of the planet was ocean. It's almost unbelievable.

Before, they had a seventh continent called Antarctica. Now it was just bedrock way below sea level. We didn't have any place on earth with natural ice anymore, it sounded cool. I thought it would've been nice to have things like snow.

I was startled out of my day dreams by a door hissing and sliding open. It was my mother half way across the house. Since she was up, I should've been too, I got up and walked to my closet. It had the same thick plastic curtain that every other house in Society would have.

That would be another nice thing, I thought it would be nice to know that my curtains could be different from our neighbors. Nope. That was being greedy. Be a happy little human with your ugly little curtains.

I walked through the plastic that fell in strips from the top of my doorway. I stood in the middle of a large room that was nearly empty of clothes. I had only a small section on the shelves to my right of folded white shirts and pants. The same clothes that everyone else in the world had. Unfortunate, I know. But even more unfortunate was that everyone else covered up their clothes with their cutesy Profiles. Not me, I actually wore the white fabric that was specially designed to be as light as possible because of the unbearable heat of our planet during the day, the dome basically circulated air, it could still get pretty warm. These supposedly light temperature controlling clothes were shoved into a corner of my closet. But sometimes I made those shirts and pants into other things. I borrowed a Seamer from Daffs' mom, it's a machine that tests the materials of materials then finds their melting points and quickly and Seamlessly, attaches them together. I had tried to make a pocket, but to cover my head, but as I held it up, it looked more like a lump of sadness. I balled it up and threw it in the corner.

My closet shouldn't have really been called a closet because it was more like a work station.

I had turned a long, low shelf into a desk; which was where I had another notebook, and pen, along with the Seamer, and broken bits of things I'd collected. Then I had rows of shelves filled with plastic tablets and tools.

That's where I stored all the things I had bought with my allowance. I saved them until I could make another trip to Medi to deliver them. My mom thought I was really into languages like she was, well she was into learning bits and pieces of French.

She had bought a tablet on beginners French. She now impressed her competition (aka neighbors or other fellow humans) by walking up to them and introducing herself in French or throwing in phrases that always received "oohs," and "ahhs." I thought she was lucky that no one understood her.

People would spew out the "bonjour's" or "comment t'appel tu's," then back out of the I-know-more-than-you-competition because my mom usually had the means to outdo people with her purchased knowledge. Even if they knew beginning words, she continued the conversation to a point where she was throwing out weirdly conjugated words to make her French skills seem never-ending. So far she hadn't been discovered, but it was only a matter of time before she was. I could tell it was going to happen, soon. Like "How is the weather today?" "Dogs on wednesday eat handing hair."

Most people couldn't afford an entire French tablet, and if they could they usually weren't able to finish and learn all the phrases or words that my mom could. I just couldn't get over the fact that she didn't learn it. I learned it just because and I practiced with Daff every once in a while, teaching her words and phrases.

I was out the front door and focusing on the hard white ground as I tried to convert my thoughts into French. I tried to distract myself so I didn't get pulled into the swirling vortex in my head that was labeled 'Unfairness of Society.'

As Preps, we had spent *several* years in school going over how to use tablets. Those are some of the beginning things that you had to go through in elementary school. Basically in kindergarten you learn how everything works, later on—if you're lucky enough, you learn why.

Chapter 6

· · · · · · · · · · · ·

Ever since elementary school I knew that I had made a mistake

by trying to stick with Tal. I should've taken the test and not tried

to hold back—assuming that I *had* actually held something back.

But I made the mistake of choosing to do anything to have a friend

since I was insecure because of my home life or whatever. Anyway,

Tal's love and affection was something that could be easily bought.

She would give it away to whomever paid the most attention. She's

a narcissist (another label from the Psychological Profiles and

Tendencies tablet).

I was feeling like a bomb, Teak had set the timer, and all of this

stuff inside of me was going to explode. I had never exploded before per say, and I was curious to see what would happen. But I had to be on my best behavior for Teakster. *I mean seriously,* he was named after a type of *wood.*

How was he the President?

"Hey Jess!" The volatile being in question walked over and smiled brightly. Apparently this week's Trend was fangs and horns. Tal wouldn't be outdone Trend-wise, so she had long thick horns that curled up and around her head, they probably would've been heavy if they were real. She was on the tame side of the Trend with only two sharp teeth(tusks) that tucked gently over her top lip. If those had been real it probably would've been hard to talk. But they weren't—Real, that is.

I gave a small smile back. "Did you hear about Savana?" My smile turned into a grimace. *Don't talk please. Just for once stop talking.* She didn't even bother to look around to check for eavesdroppers. She knew they were listening.

"It's so sad really," *I guess we're talking*. She made her enormous violet eyes wider. "She wore scales," Tal said offhandedly, like "Oh, what can you expect from someone like *that?*"

Tal and Savana had a falling out when Savana started spreading all of these rumors about me and how I didn't wear a profile because I had committed some crime. Tal called her out on it, in a big way. At first it reminded me why we were friends, but I kind of realized she could have done it just for the attention and Popularity Votes. So for the past couple months, I had been extra helpful and disgustingly supportive to make up for it, but I was done. I felt a gentle warmth coming from my wrist accompanied by a flashing white light, the Weekly Update. I quickly opened my Profile with my index and thumb pinched then quickly spread them apart. A purple haze clouded my vision and slowly settled to become the background to the Leaderboard. On the right half of my vision was the Academics Leaderboard.

I watched the slots slowly fill in one by one. I irritatedly scrolled to the top of the list with my ghostly hands that showed up in my Profile. I knew that my Real hands would have stayed in the same position they were before I had opened my Profile. I looked to the first slot and saw JESSICA FINCHE. That was normal, I looked to the first Leaderboard labeled Popularity, this was first for a reason. No matter how smart you are, it doesn't mean people will vote for you. You had to be in the top 10 slots on both Leaderboards to have any political potential. If you aren't in the top 10, then you won't get the top government positions—the best jobs Preps could get. And everyone wanted the top slots. The top jobs came with the most benefits, money, power, everything. I could count my actual competitors on one hand. Savana, her minion, and Tal being the biggest. I was fine with being President, or even Vice. But there was no way I would settle for anything less. I finished scrolling to the top and I looked at the first five slots. I wasn't there. I scrolled down faster to the top seven, not there either. I slowly scrolled down to the tenth person on the list. I wasn't there. I scrolled back and checked frantically. I let out a breath slowly. I scrolled down until the numbers almost hit twenty. JESSICA FINCHE was across the seventeenth slot. I felt my head pounding, and fluttering in my stomach. I had never gone below tenth before. Ever. My rank had slowly been dropping, but I had no idea what would push me out of the top 10. I shakily closed my Profile and looked at Tal, who was in the middle of a story.

It was *so* boring, but it distracted me for a moment. My neck ached with nodding along so much that I had just stopped. Tal didn't pay attention anyway. I wondered if these kinds of things happened in Medi or Accel, probably. But I liked to think that they didn't.

"You aren't even listening to me, are you?" Tal turned and looked at me. I started to say something then stopped.

"You okay?" Her flawless feather eyebrows jumped to the top of her forehead. I thought about it for a second and said, "Nothing that's within the realm of fixable." She smirked, "So definitely Broken then?" I nodded and looked around distractedly.

I regretted telling Tal about the 'categories' I had made in my head. Whenever you see something new and sleek—or not, you say so and put it in a category. She loved it, and when she used it, it made me feel bad that I have even started it. Which was a rude thing for her to do. I felt like if I told Tal stuff, she'd tweak it a bit, and make it kind of, Trendy. I hated that. But it was exactly what I needed.

"Tal,"

"Yeah?"

"I want to be back in the top 10." I looked at her. I saw her eyes drift, she quickly scanned the Leaderboards and was back.

"It's fixable." I smiled gratefully.

"But first you need to change, before, you were aloof, kind of interesting you had that going for you with the whole Profile thing. But now you're boring, something happened. And they need to see you differently. You need to start Campaigning." My smile froze on my face. I knew what Campaigning was. I didn't want to do it. After Prep, there's a career assigning term. Everything from your history, your rankings and Campaigning history will allow you to qualify for the top slots, even if you're ranked first, you have to undergo extensive interviews and then the larger public voting. Usually there are only three candidates. I was going to be one of those three.

"We can start today. But first we'll decide on what your angle is." I didn't want to be a figurehead. That's what Campaigning is. You give people an idea, and they follow if they like the idea. It's like a costume. And I didn't want to put it on.

"You'll still be in the running, you have two years of school left, you've had two solid years as a base. It's only natural you would change your persona and grow." I was going to put on the mask.

I didn't say anything. All around the entrance there were swishing tails and hands covering whispers. I braced myself to put on my school disguise. I had decided that with different kinds of people, they could only deal with certain kinds of Jess. With Tal, I could be the snarkier, funnier, wittier Jess. That way I could kind of blend with the rest of the Preps, but I was always quicker than them. I think that's what Tal liked and she claimed me as her friend.

I didn't know if I would have to be more of Tals' Jess. I sighed, I had to get serious if I really wanted to change my rank. I needed to focus on school, but the popularity department specifically. I liked the learning part of school. It's just too bad we didn't do very much of it, and even more of a pity it wasn't that important.

We strolled through the long front hallway. I was too distracted to count all 34 steps that it took to get to the first door on the left. I was too worn out to be annoyed that 34 was a totally random number, it would've made so much more sense just to round it off to 35 or 40, but *no*. 34 sounded much more... *logical*. It's a good thing no one had obsessive compulsive disorders or they'd be crying on the steps.

I waited for the door to slide open after I had pushed my thumb on the finger scanner which was slightly sticky. I impatiently waited for the headache-inducing blue light to pulse over my thumb. After it scanned it, I scowled, *disgusting*. I roughly wiped my thumb on my shirt and after giving an exasperated sigh, I used the corner of my shirt to wipe the scanner clean. I heard people behind me murmuring. I ignored them. *No wonder you're seventeenth.* I ground my teeth.

Once we walked in I went to the front and sat on a hard blue chair. Tal and I would probably be the only people in the front. It was a weird habit I had started and she had joined in on. Usually I got to class early to "go over" the class material with the teacher. Tal told me I was wasting my time and that our Educators were incompetent, she didn't actually want to learn, she just liked being adverse. I had kind of blown off the teacher, I'd probably have to stay after. *Ick.* Basically she asked me questions about the material, she was nice, just not…..*good.*

In the next minute, every student walked through the door including Savanna and her Vice, Os. Savana looked at me then tossed her head, to show off her lavender horns peeking over light cream feather hair, and smirked, Os had matching colored feathers and set his sloping jaw as he strode to his seat. I didn't comment and Tal looked taken aback. I looked away. I wasn't really in the mood to laugh at one of her stupid snarky remarks. I was sizing up the competition, I had never considered them as that before. Before they were just a nuisance.

She was dangerous.

Savana was ranked first. A different guy was second. He wasn't an actual competitor, because he didn't want to win. Tal was third. Os was ninth, unimportant. I looked into Savana's eyes until she looked away. *I'm not losing to her.*

I looked up as Educator Levy walked in. She smiled at the class and looked slightly deranged. Educator Levy was, nicely put— unique. She opted out of using a Profile for her face, but used it to keep the rest of her body looking "young". She was a really sweet lady, but she was the last person who should have ever been an Educator. I usually was pretty accepting and thought that it was just her own way at making herself unique, today, it made me uncomfortable. I probably wouldn't have even argued if Tal had started with the insults.

I shifted in my seat. You couldn't be both, she needed to pick one. Tal agreed with me on that part. She was in the -ish category. Which was not even a thing.

"Alrighty class," her voice cracked and I winced. My school demeanor was falling apart at the seams.Calm, cool, and collected was seeping over to the nervous, neurotic, and non-important side of the emotional spectrum.

"Can anyone guess what the *most* important period of history was?" She got a few glares in response. Tal included. Out of the corner of my eye, I saw her horns discreetly turning from the emerald green they had been to a deep shade of periwinkle. Her horns were fluctuating between that and violet. I didn't have to look over at Savanna to notice her horns had been purple, Tal was that predictable, and I knew she had liked the color and wanted it, but she had to choose something that was Trendy and not an obvious imitation of Savanna.

"Good answer, you're right, and why is it the most important? Because it made us who we are today." I looked down at the desk made of the same screen as tablets. They were like the most basic versions of tablets available, and half of the time didn't work. I looked down and caught a glimpse of a poorly pieced together timeline.

	Green Age 2070+		Profiles were legalized 2150	
Dark Age 2030+		Change Age 2100+		Tracks were forn 2151

"It was indeed the Green Age." She looked smug. She usually was unsure in teaching. *And she should be. Worst timeline ever.*

"The Green Age was when all the politicians and all the civilians, and all the people of the world realized that, *they,* were killing their planet during the Dark Age." I scoffed quietly and tapped on the top right corner twice then swirled my fingers around the middle to open the free space section of the tablet. I tapped Tal and drew a circle at the top that said ALL THE PEOPLE OF THE WORLD then I drew one arrow pointing to CIVILIANS and another to POLITICIANS. Then the side note said; Apparently hard to differentiate.

Tal snorted and blinked three times, when she looked away I saw the reflection of the desk was still in her eyes. I hissed at her. She looked back and I exaggerated my lips as I mouthed, "Shot Updates?" She nodded smugly and I leaned back. I noticed the reflection soon left her eyes but suddenly the rest of the class abruptly laughed then stopped as Levy glared manically at us until we were quiet.

I smiled as I noticed Savanna glared at Tal. It was hard to know when people were Inline, but there were few occasions when they were messaging each others Profiles that it became obvious. Apparently, Tal would be the topic of the day. My smile dropped as I got slightly annoyed with Tal. I needed a higher ranking, not her. I directed my irritation at the teacher as Educator Levy trudged on.

"So they dedicated to finding new sources of energy like water energy, and wind energy; which are what sustains today's society. Since the average temperature rose from 58 degrees to 80, it created currents that only benefit and strengthen us." She her hands fluttered as she spoke, "Those currents are savage and—and rough! And we—we convert them into energy that we use. Since those currents are *so* strong we have enough to power everything we need!"

I thought I saw her eye twitch every time her voice rose an octave, *maybe she was terminal.* "Since the temperatures rose so much, our wind also became stronger and so we built wind tunnels and turbines and now we have more than enough energy for anything we want. It's just up to Accel to build things to use all that harnessed energy!" She ended happily. I couldn't tell how many times she had practiced this speech before class. That was the most put together she had ever been, like... *ever.* After I joined the class in a moment of stunned silence, I took a second to process what she had just finished saying.

You've got to be kidding me. There had to be some kind of balance, either sub-par teaching or mediocre teaching of trash. *What, is it going to snow tomorrow too?* I laughed. I realized I laughed out loud, I felt the blood drain from my face. *You're so dead.*

Her smile froze on her face. "And what exactly is so funny about Society's *amazing* history, miss Finche?" she asked sharply. Tal bit back her smile as she stayed silent. I glared at her for a moment then looked at Levy.

Seriously? Well, the lesson made sense if the class was called; "Deceive Your Peers," *Well, peers is a stretch*. If it was like "make up your own world day," yeah, she aced that.

"The Green Age started because our ancestors ran out of coal aka the "Dark Age," they had no power, no fuel. That's it, they didn't stop out of kindness, it was because over the years they had gotten greedier and greedier and started digging up more and more coal, and used it faster than they found it. And one day, *poof!* It all went away." I hadn't realized I was talking until I noticed my hands clenched in my lap as I started spewing out the contents of my last two history tablets. I wanted to stop but there was something inside me that pushed the words out of my mouth.

I started talking faster, "The world plummeted for years, then they saw the aftermath. The water levels rose, the temperatures rose, people near the old line in the middle of the planet called the equator died because it was so hot. People along the coastlines drowned. Almost all the animals in the oceans died, and the ones that were left were fought over until they—we—the *stupid humans* killed all the animals too. That's why we have to eat that disgusting tofu and live at the tippy-top of the planet. Because they killed everything else. I just think it's funny you think that's good." I finished quietly. I knew I was in trouble. So much trouble. But it just felt *so great* to be right, and tell her that she was wrong. I had always kind of wondered when I would snap at her grating voice asking stupid questions, or when I would get fed up at her answering my questions with, "well, it's because it was made that way."

I expected the others to laugh like they had before, but the class was silent., their feathers rustled without a breeze or sound. They wouldn't do anything until they saw who won, and some were too preoccupied with growing modest horns on the middle of their hair to pay attention. That's how everyone in Prep was for moment, I had forgotten. They waited to see who the winner was to cheer for them, or they were too busy to watch the fight. I felt gross that I had actually cared about their opinions for a second.

"Did you get your information from a *history tablet* miss Finche?" I thought I had seen hurt flash across her muddy eyes. I must have imagined it, since a second later, her features hardened over to a cold mask as she sneered like I had done something inferior. I ignored the fact that my face burned.

I swallowed and tensed the sides of my face. It was my way of forcibly making myself emotionless, I could tell it wasn't working since my face was heating up. "Yes."

"Well, I suppose you weren't satisfied by my teaching you, is that it?" she asked so that it sounded like she was talking to a little kid. Saccharine, that's the word.

I didn't answer and looked down at my hands which were now gripping the sides of the blue chair. *No. I just actually want to know more than, oh, our ancestors had all this lovely food blah, blah, blah. But*

we have tofu. Don't ask why. We just have it. Just be happy not *knowing.*

"Hmm, well since you have *blatantly showed,* that you think I'm

not a qualified teacher you can go home now." I gently lifted my

fingers off the edges of the chair. And felt tears start to form.

I frowned and blinked harshly, what, *leave early?*

"Yes, I do mean it, grab your bag and go home and think about

what respect looks like." She told me, still using the sickly sweet

voice.

"But I was just saying that you weren't right about—"

"Please leave. Now miss Finche!" She screeched at me. I forced

a smirk and slowly looked down at my desktop and entered a

pattern that set the mainframe to a black screen. I got out of my

chair slowly and forced myself to look at her.

"Oh, I think it's broken, you might have to…call in a *Medi* to help you, since you wouldn't be able to do it yourself, *would you?*" I felt her eyes on me but I looked straight ahead and walked towards the door. I heard people laughing, along with a few cheers behind me, and one of the girls ask why she didn't get to go home.

Respect is a word.

She should have said "Think about what respect means and how you didn't show it today. Then think about how in the future you can show respect." That would've been a much better answer. *Once again she's shown herself to be incompetent. That's all that proves.*

I felt like poking her eye with my finger. Well, maybe not my because that would've felt gross and gotten eye juice under my nail.

Levy was not, in fact qualified to be an Educator. *Seriously? Way to be a prime example for education Levy. Whooop! Students interested in learning, nope, better scream at them for participating. That's a great plan.*

I was about ready to kill whoever decided that the people who didn't make the cut for government positions should work with teaching "tomorrows future." Teak was doing a trash job of—

I felt an angry throb starting behind my eyes, if Teak found out about this… *Oh I'm so dead.*

I dragged my feet home away from the grey mass of school. Home was around 15 minutes away at the slowest amble possible. All of the homes were in the same relative area so that all the people hiding their gasping selves behind Profiles could walk there and back with minimal effort. As I walked further, I moved my hands from the milky white guard railing that differentiated the street from the hazards like broken street, or dirt, which was viewed as having the potential for severe danger.

I usually walked along the outside of the thick tubes that guided the pedestrian traffic just to be rebellious and all that, I just wasn't in the mood. I started thinking of L, and felt a smile tug the corner of my lips, as I held the seamless guard rail. He would've done the thing, where he would just lean back and sigh to try and cover a smile. I knew that was exactly what he would've done if he had been in the class. And L would've walked out with me.

As I walked along I started to pay attention to the signs. They were the same thick tubes standing up, with dark tablets with singular programs had arrows and labels which told you were you were. The next sign I saw was labeled MEDI in thick letters. I slowed my pace but ended up walking past the street that lead to Medi. I thought about going to talk to him, but I realized, with Teak and all, I would get to talk to them everyday soon enough.

I walked up to my front door and glared at it. It was so close, but I really didn't want to go inside. If I did that I knew I would never want to come back out. I glared harder. "I hate you so much," I lifted a finger and stabbed the door. I clenched my teeth and quickly went inside the house. I rushed into my closet, grabbed my handmade jacket, and shoved all the tablets in sight into my bag, then I ran back out. I was going to do it.

"Why not make my day even more memorable? Get kicked out of school, then kicked out of my Track too." I grumbled. I pushed back my hair and took a deep breath, I'd done this before, but I'd never had any consequences for doing it.

Do it.

The controversy was halted when I felt a sharp tug, and realized my fingers were tangled in my pin-straight hair. I untangled it and made a plan.

I started walking toward the Medi district.

I pulled my hood up higher to cover my knotted white hair. I'd

thought about changing my Profile to see what I'd look like with

brown hair, but I decided if I wanted different colored hair, I was

going to dye it. It would still be fake, but in a more Real way.

I had decided that the one benefit to having Preps a leaders, was

that they were incredibly meticulous. They divided the space inside

the dome into fourths, one quarter for each track, and the last was

Head Quarters, where Profiles and banks were operated from. I

looked around to see homes with the same layout as the ones in

Prep, just smaller. It was more cozy that way., they had the same

amount of space we had, Medis were just more efficient. They were

still all the same color, which was a bummer. But the people were

better than in Prep.

Maybe it wouldn't be so bad to be in Medi.

Everyone had a job. Some families were Growers; they grew the

different ingredients to make the tofu that sustained our

population. Then the Makers actually made the food. Then there were families that were the upper class of Medi, like Q and L's family. They were the Fixers. Anytime there was a problem with the turbines or waterwheels, they went out to where they were and fixed the problem. They all had a purpose. In Prep, people were just....there. I mean sure, they were Politicians, but all of the people who didn't qualify for politics became Educators. No one in Prep was very, altering. Medis changed they way we lived and Preps just, took.

I walked past the three different rows of houses to get to the fourth—where Q and L lived. Daff too. There were more people in Medi than in Prep and Accel combined, so it was a lot of walking. I finally reached the plain house with the average beige door. I knocked twice. The door slid open with a sad creak, and I suppressed a smile as I heard yelling from inside the house.

I hadn't realized I was sweating until I took off my jacket and it was damp underneath my arms and behind my neck. I knew that my shirt would be stained, I stood uncomfortably and crossed my arms.

"Jess!" I heard a yell. I didn't fight the smile that took over my face. I stepped back from the force of a fourteen year old ball of energy with brown hair that ran toward me.

"Hi," She was out of breath. Her shimmering brown eyes were excited.

"Guess what," Daff could barely contain herself.

"What? Did Q take a mirror out of his room?" I played along.

She snorted and smirked. "Not nearly as drastic."

I laughed, "What then?"

"Mom's finally letting me go on a Fixing with L and Q!" My smile froze on my face.

Daff didn't notice. "They said it wasn't going to be a wheel job," I relaxed slightly. Working with water wheels, in rivers or oceans, was one of the most dangerous types of jobs a Fixer could go on. Unfortunately, Daff wanted *only* the dangerous jobs. Which was really admirable actually, but I didn't want her going in Fixings. At all. She had worked on her strength with Q ever since I had met her, trying to prove that even though she was small, she could get big stuff done. At the time, it was irritatingly impressive, even more irritating to be reminded that she wanted it so badly.

"I'm just going to get to go on a turbine job. But it's ok, eventually I'll get to go do something exciting." She was nearly bouncing up and down. *Wind turbines?* I saw Q walk around his little sister and nod at me. L bounded up behind him.

"Hi," He said, sharing the same dark eyes as his sister. He smiled and his whole face lit up when he did.

"Hi," I said flatly. His face fell slightly. Then he quickly looked at Daff, a look of understanding crossed his face.

"Daff's pumped for her first Fixing," I stared at him until he had the decency to look uncomfortable, "It's going to be with turbines, Jess," He said it gently, "She's going to have to do it eventually," He finished softly. I made my face harden and watched his relaxed facade start to crack.

I flicked a strand of hair out of my face and looked at Daff, "If you promise to be careful, I have a few presents to give you." Her eyebrows jumped and I saw the notorious spark light up her eyes.

She looked at me intensely and pulled me down several centimeters, so she could whisper in my ear. I grunted from the force she used to pull me down, I had forgotten that although she was small, she was tough.

"Watch it and be nice, he can't fix it." I bit the inside of my cheek and hugged her lithe frame closely. As I rested my head on her neck

she breathed into my ear, "And neither can you." My body stiffened and I held her tighter. She shook me off and stood up taller.

"Ok, ok." She rushed to say, gluing her excited face back on, "I promise," I brought myself back to the present and pulled the first tablet out of my bag. I hadn't even thought about which ones I grabbed when I had rushed out of the house. The tablet I had pulled out was the French tablet. I rushed to think of something as I looked down at the screen.

"So when you're on jobs, you and your.. *letters*, can talk," Q snorted acting outraged, "And no one will know what you're saying," She smirked at Q and nodded, happy that she would be able to learn more than just bits and pieces of a language. She laid her hand on it. I had deactivated the motion openings, they were too complicated to remember. Daff tapped the screen twice as she slowly walked over to the couch. A tablet took up your entire line of sight the same way a Profile did. So all we saw was Daff smiling and a dark screen. I turned to L with my hand in my bag.

"You don't have to do this you know," He smiled gently.

"It's the only way I can help L, so I do it, plus now you and Daff can make fun of all the Preps." I said quietly looking over at the engrossed girl in question.

He touched my shoulder gently and I felt my skin hum. I dropped my shoulder and his hand slipped off, my skin felt warm, "Well I just want to say thanks, thanks so much Jess," I rearranged my face into a smile and nodded.

I cleared my throat, "I have like ten of these soooo, is this going to be a long process, or…"

"Oh, no," He laughed and pushed back his dark hair, and I noticed the subtle contrast of his nails against his skin, "Here, we can set them on the table." We moved over toward the cluttered table that he hastily cleared off.

He was setting a container on the other counter when he turned to look at me. I realized how close his face was and backed up imperceptibly. "Do you want something to drink? When's the last time you had some water?" His eyes searched my face accusingly.

"I'm fine," I brushed him off, "Thanks, but I finished another bottle at school." He raised his eyebrows and didn't say anything.

I took out the tablets and rambled out the name of each one.

"Ok, Machinery, the basics,"

"Sweet."

"Oh and the funniest thing happened today," I pulled out another tablet.

"What? Kind of a shady title."

"Not a title, it's a Jess Story; I got kicked out, for knowing too much stuff," I kept my head facing my bag.

"Get out!" I could hear L's smile.

I grinned back, "I already did."'

He laughed and I continued setting tablets on the table.

"Climate Change, History in a Nutshell, Bad Jokes, Psychology 101,"

"Less exciting," The corner of his mouth lifted, I rolled my eyes.

"Best TV Shows of the 2030's,"

"And as fascinating as that sounds, context."

I looked , "They're kind of like stories, or the visuals that are in tablets sometimes,"

L nodded, "Oh, Ok,"

"Yeah," I scratched my arm monitor absently.

"Are you ok with getting kicked out?" He asked as he turned his back to me and started putting utensils in the Cleaner.

I didn't answer for a second, "I'm not, actually. I didn't think I would even care. But I do, and I'm not ok with it. Because it means I'm out of Prep, for sure." I finished setting the tablets on the table. "It's—bad this time, I don't know if I'll be able to get out of this one." The words left a bitter taste in my mouth.

"I'm sorry Jess, but at least you'll be rid of Preps for good right? You won't have to deal with them anymore." *What he means is you won't have to deal with having an intense career.*

I didn't have to hide my expression since he was turned around,"Yeah, I think you're right," I said, feeling something very close to disappointment. He knew how much being President meant to me. He knew how important it was that I ran for office, no one else would ever make any real changes.

"Clothes of Everyday Folk, Household Pets, Continents and Oceans, aannnnnd, that's it." I looked down at the stack, it had felt like I had brought over a lot more. I turned around to check that I hadn't left any in the bag when I felt arms wrapped around my torso.

I held my breath. L shifted away uncomfortably and ran his hand through his hair. I scratched my neck and groaned inside. I could tell his face was heating up, just like mine did when I was being exceptionally awkward. I punched his shoulder and opened my arms as I made big sweeping gestures. He grinned and shook his head as he wrapped his arms around me again, "You know, you're really good at making people uncomfortable," his voice grumbled in my ear. I laughed and shook him off, L's eyes were suddenly drawn to his wrist.

His arm monitor flashed and I averted my eyes. I gave a silent thanks to whoever broke a wind turbine, and felt bad afterwards. "Well, I'd better get going, right?" I spoke to an unresponsive L. I walked up and tapped his shoulder for conformation. "That's what I should, yeah ok, I'm going now."

I waved to Daff who was too busy with her French tablet to notice. Q saluted me and gave a whispered, "Thanks!" as he discretely walked behind L to grab what I was pretty sure was the Household Pets tablet. *Interesting choice.*

I looked around the house for the last time. *I guess I could live here. Well not here, here, I mean in Medi.* I took one last glance before I turned, grabbed my jacket, and walked out the door.

I trudged back to my house thinking about life in Medi. They always had three children as a minimum to sustain the work force. That would mean a family, and partnering with someone in Medi. *I don't want kids.* A sibling maybe, but no kids, I wouldn't know the first thing about them. And I didn't really want to partner with anyone in Medi either. *Even L?* I ignored the voice in my head.

I walked back out the way I came but instead of turning left and heading back to school, I hesitated only for a second before I turned right, toward the building. I decided that if I was already getting

kicked out, I should try and make the most of my situation.

Chapter 7

. . . .

My legs throbbed in memory of my last visit, and I made sure to watch where I stepped. I carefully wrapped my hands around one of the more stable looking parts of the fence. As I took a deep breath and lifted my left leg over, my toes searched for footing. Once I finally found a patch of flat rocks that I set my weight on. I let out the breath I had been holding in and stood straddling the fence. I swung my other leg over and let go. I looked at the building and my feet dejectedly trudged on.

It was dangerous work; there were stones jutting out from the ground trying to put an abrupt halt to my journey. My steps slowed once I stood in front of the dome doors. I looked up to see rounded edges that would gently slide a clear, rounded door, in between to panes of translucent plastic. The doors were reinforced with bars that crossed protectively around the inside, and there was little support to bar things from outside. I adjusted the Oxy-Pack I was relieved I had remembered to bring. I dried my moist hand on my pants and lifted up the cover on the panel with only two buttons. One was clear and the other was black, I pushed my thumb on the clear one and held my thumb still while it was scanned. It took a while to get a defined print, but once it did, the doors whooshed open.

It took me at least an hour to get to the building, between blocking the sun from my face, and gulping down my Oxy-Pack. I could've read half of a tablet in that time. Throughout the walk, my brain could only come up with a very limited selection of topics to think of. The major one being death, the second being ways I could die.

I started filing my head with ideas of dead bodies. What if the building was where they hid all the dead bodies? *You don't even know what a dead body looks like.*

I knew that in the years before the Green Age, billions of people had died. It's sad but it was mostly the people who survived that were causing the problems in the first place.

We were at the top of the planet where there weren't that many people to begin with. *They don't put dead bodies in a building.* That would be unsafe, and it would smell horrible. Plus, they would make the building uglier if it had dead people inside.

I had all these thoughts spinning around in my head while I was walking. I was so distracted that I didn't realize I had reached the building until I had walked past it.

I had looked up and panicked. *Aaaaannnd, you're going to die out here. Hey, now you'll be the dead body in the middle of nowhere.* I could hear my heartbeat in my ears. I turned my head left and right but I couldn't find the building. *Say goodbye.* My mouth was getting dry. I was going to shrivel up and die. *Goodbye tofu, good bye stupid righteous teachers, goodbye —*

I spun around to retrace my steps and found myself staring at a shimmering blue door. My heart was still pounding from the scare of being out there. I couldn't imagine myself ten steps away, dead. Cause of death; stupidity. The building I had been staring at for months was right in front of me.

I moved closer to the door and hesitantly swiped at it. The image was clear, but my hand went clear through it. I growled. *Great plan, now what?* I thought, my teeth clenched. I could close my eyes. I thought about it and nodded. Otherwise the buildings' Profile would just give me a headache. I let out a breath and closed my eyes. I stuck my arms out and started moving them in sweeping gestures. My arms hit a wall. I pressed my palms flat against it and slowly shuffle to the side. After a a while, I found what felt like a door, but with a handle. I grabbed what I hoped was a handle. It was disgusting. The handle was rough, hot, and felt like it could cut open my hand and puke puss into it. *That was graphic.* I pushed against the door but it didn't budge. I pulled, it still wouldn't open.

"Are you serious?" I asked the doorI peeked an eye open and wished I hadn't, instead of a door, there was just dark empty space, the Programmers probably didn't think anyone would actually go out here . I clenched my fists. I noticed my wrist was blinking. I turned it over, closed my eyes, and kept talking. *I don't want to find out.*

"Okay, fine, I'm just going to walk around, be passive aggressive until I figure out a solution." I muttered, then I started shuffling around the building.

"All the while narrating my thoughts, because that's what'll make this memorable," I grumbled.

I decided I would inspect it first, before I got too hasty.

"Ow," I had tried to tap it lightly with my foot, but I had swung my leg too aggressively.

"Well, if the building is this old, it doesn't matter as long as the floor and supports are stable," I was pretty good at sounding like I knew what I was talking about. I was trying to talk myself into forgetting how old the structure probably was.

"Today has just been an extraordinary day. I'm getting kicked out, of basically everything. And my mouth feels slightly chalky." I swallowed dryly and decided the narration could continue internally. So far, not the *worst* day ever.

I found an opening, my arms had flapped at the sudden ending of the wall.

It wasn't the door. It was a ledge that went to my waist. It felt like I would have to pull myself on the ledge then slide in. My lip curled at the thought of all the dust and grime that I could feel rolling under my hands. My mouth then fell into a frown as I reached up and felt something hanging overhead that creaked as I touched it.

The thing was felt like a metal door with different panels that were on a… track?I risked opening my eyes and saw exactly what I was feeling. I suspiciously touched the panels above my head again, *definitely there. Weird.* It was very weird, I tried to move on. It looked like that the door had been pulled up on the track so it was hanging from the top of the ceiling.

I squinted my eyes, the door-thing seemed like it could snap shut at any second. I *really* wanted to look inside, but that thing looked unstable. *As you swing your leg up onto the ledge—CRUNCH, that was the bone in your leg shattering into millions of tiny pieces, then-*

I took a deep breath in, and tried not to think about anything regarding doors, legs, loud noises, or pain. The leg crunching kept on popping into my head. Each version more gruesome than the last.

I let out my breath. I was a little light headed. I needed to sit down.

I walked over to the ledge, it didn't matter if snapped shut anymore, it just mattered that I didn't pass out from the heat.

My vision smudged at the edges, and everything was tilting back and forth. My mouth felt dryer than before as I sat down, and heard a loud noise. It was like something was scraping against the floor of the building, I tried to ignore it as I reached for the ledge. My hands grasped for the edges of it. *Finally!* I gave a lopsided grin as I reached it and felt the cold rough concrete against my hand. It felt great.

My grin dropped as I heard that noise again. It was a loud scrape, and I could feel it dragging across my skull. I grabbed my ears to try and make it go away. It was one of those obnoxious, conceited noises, banging, doing whatever it wanted while other people were trying to not pass out. Very inconsiderate. I heard it again but this time it was more of a high pitched screech. I groaned. I slowly dropped my hands as everything started looking differently than it had before.

I lifted up my arms and looked at them; it didn't feel like I had lifted them up, it felt like I was wearing my Profile. It was like my brain was telling me, if I fell, it wouldn't hurt. *But what if I fell on something really sharp?* My brain tried to tell me it would feel nice. *But what if it was really sharp, like a sideways table, that was also pointy?* My brain said that would never happen so I should just fall down already. I lifted the mouthpiece that connected to my Oxy-Pack and took a long breath. It felt cool on my throat, but made me realize how dry my throat was.

I was thirsty. *Maybe I can fall down after a drink?* I remembered I hadn't taken any water with me when I came back from school.

I felt my heart pound sluggishly as I realized it. I hadn't had anything to drink for several hours and then I had the brilliant idea of walking for more than a kilometer when it was more than 96 degrees outside.

"Jess!" I tired to yell. This was one of the first lessons that they drill into you since kindergarten. We were taught that we had to drink 12 cups of water a day on average ever since the temperatures had risen. We had to drink more so that our bodies could continue to function and stay cool. But I hadn't done that. Because I was stupid. *Really* stupid. L had even offered. *Not thinking about it.*

I still had my shaky hand on the ledge. I lifted my eyes and decided to climb on it.

I lifted my leg, and once it touched the cold floor of the building, I felt like I was going to lose my balance. I set my face on the coolness and stayed still. Everything was swirling around inside my head, so I shut my eyes. *At least it didn't crush my leg.*

As I turned my head, I saw the inside of the building and two silver blocks right in front of my face. I felt my eyes widen as I realized I could've hit my head. *Nice one, nearly die of dehydration then finish the job by smashing my head.* I reached my hand out to them; I wanted to see if they were colder than the floor. They weren't. They were squishy when I dropped my hand on them. I moaned as they started moving. The blocks backed up and I put my hands over my head.

Not only was I dying, I was seeing things now, too. My throat felt raw, but I forgot about it once I saw a face with brown hair lean down over the blocks.

The face grew arms then that started tugging on me until I felt my other leg land on the ledge, and I was being dragged away.

Chapter 8

· · · · · · · · · · ·

"You shouldn't be out here without water you know," The voice

seared behind my face and across my skull.

My head felt sore and my throat was worse.

I opened my eyes to see a gray swirling mass of sky framed by

protruding poles and crumbling cement.

My head throbbed as I sat up. I heard footsteps walk over. I

craned my head around to see, and a sharp pain went up it. I

moaned.

"Oh please, the pity ship has sailed, you shouldn't have been

out here in the first place, anyway, how did you get an invitation?"

I looked up and saw a girl with brown hair.

She crouched down, pulled out a bottle from a smooth sack that I tried to catch a glimpse of, and screwed off the lid. She handed it to me and when I didn't reach out to take it, raised her eyebrows and shook it.

I heard something slosh around so I put out my hand and she smirked and set it down, I glared at her.

"Whaaarrr." I started coughing. I brought the bottle up to my lips and took a quick sip. I sighed, the water felt nice as it trickled down my throat. I took a second gulp, which irritated my throat and made me start coughing again.

She smirked, "So how did you get an invitation?" I pushed my eyebrows together after my coughing fit had ended. "You aren't in Accel, are you? I haven't seen you around. I would remember if I've seen you before." I tried to be offended, but I didn't feel up to it. So I settled for irritation instead.

"No no no!" She quickly put out her hands, "not in a "you're absurdly ugly" way or anything, it's just that I remember everything." I glared.

Not only was she rude, she was in Accel. Which was a very bad combination.

I remembered that Accels are usually what people like to call "gifted." From what I could tell so far, they were just awkward and rude, gifted was sounding like a bit of a stretch. But the rest of the myths had yet to be disproved. Accels apparently didn't stoop to the same lowly levels as the rest of us. They weren't occupied with frivolities like looks or careers.

This girl looked pretty focused on what she looked like. She had short, smooth brown hair and piercing blue eyes. She didn't have fangs though, or any horns, that was odd. It didn't look like she was following any of the Trends. When I looked closer, something was tugging in my memory, but I pushed it aside.

"Soo…If you're not here with an invitation…" Then she tilted her head, like she was waiting for me to say something.

I didn't say anything, and she just turned up the intensity of her stare. She quickly stood up and sat next to me.

"What are you—" I asked aghast. "Okay, okay, I didn't get an invitation!"

"Scooch!" She laughed but then her smile dropped after she heard what I had said. Her smile dimmed slightly.

"Then I'm going to have to bring you to the director," she looked apologetic, "Sorry but it's protocol,"

What director?

"I'm going to cut you some slack because you seem to desperately need it" She shook her head and smirked. "Ok, so, I already told her to expect you."

I looked at her, "How did you—"

"It's an Accel tool." She cut me off. *Rude.*

I started getting up. "Well listen, thanks so much, um, I don't really need to see your director, I'm on probation already so I really don't need to get in anymore trouble." I quickly backed up.

"Yeah, I know, but you're still meeting her," She shrugged.

"Yeah, ok, nice meeting you," I wasn't very good with conversations, but she was awful."And you are…" I waited for her to finish.

"Ibis," she quirked her mouth."My darling grandma fraternized with ornithologists." She left it at that.

Ornithology…. It seemed familiar… I remembered. Years ago, I had bought Tal a tablet on the study of birds. That was when beaks were all the rage. Ornithology meant birds.

"What type of bird?" I asked.

Ibis looked taken aback. Like she hadn't expected me to say that. I smirked. *Take that. Miss I-remember-everything.*

"It apparently used to be a scavenger, and would search for food in the water."

"So does that mean your parents think you're a scavenger?"

"Well, no it just means—"

I cut her off, "Is that supposed a good thing?"

"No!" Ibis dropped her usual smile. "It just means that my grandma found this bird beautiful, and my dad agreed with her and that's what he named his kid."

I shifted my weight from foot to foot. I didn't say anything and just looked around. *Cause you're a dirt sack now.* I felt bad, but she was making me meet her "director." Plus she would probably find a way to tell Teak.

I picked at the rim of the water bottle. *Don't feel guilty. Don't…* *oh, you did it.*

"I'm going to leave." I frowned as I tried to get up. What was I still doing there? I needed to leave.

"Well, ok, umm, take the water bottle with you and be careful, ok?" Ibis startled me out of my thoughts. She stretched out her arms and walked over.

"Yeah sure, ok." I mumbled as I thought about what other categories Ibis could fit in. Weird. Not Trendy. Bossy.

"See you tomorrow, you've got a meeting with—" Ibis called out as she moved the creaky door, I couldn't hear the last part.

"Mmm hmmm," I muttered distractedly. I remember turning around to tell her that no, I wouldn't see her tomorrow. When I looked out the, I saw a girl with brown hair running out of the building.

I walked out of the building and looked around. Wherever she went, she went quickly.

———————————

I stepped over the fence and walked to my house. I let out a breath I had been holding when I saw that Teak wasn't waiting outside.

I opened my front door as I promised myself I would never do anything like that ever again. I put the water bottle on the counter and looked up as I heard someone clear their throat. *So close.* He was there. Again. In my house. I grabbed my own water bottle and walked over slowly to the counter. *What do I say?* Sorry?

"Jessica," He said sternly. I cringed. His skin was orange and he had horns that were way bigger than Tal's. All his teeth were sharp and shone in the light.

"Listen Teak, I'm really sorry, I just, I didn't mean for it to happen, it's just that it's been a weird day and I—"

"You knew the consequences of your actions Miss Finche," He tried to hold down a smile that was threatening to take over his face. He really was messed up. *Well he looks the part.*

"I know, but I didn't really do anything *bad*, I haven't gone to Medi—" *That's a lie.*

"You yelled at a teacher and threatened her with your father's position!" His orange skin deepened a shade.

"I never threatened her!" I did the other part though, I clenched my fists.

He calmed down slightly. "Do you like Prep, Jessica?"

I nodded my head vigorously and dug my nails into my hand. *No, I hate it. And you.* He smiled. *I'm only there to replace you.*

"Well it's unfortunate then. You're being moved to a Track where you will learn to appreciate the way our society works. I hope you'll learn a lot." I looked at him pleadingly. He ignored me and his eyes glazed over my head. He was messaging someone. Ibis did the same thing.

"Oh, and one last thing, please meet a girl named Ibis tomorrow for re-testing, she said she knows where to find you." He winked one heavy eyelid weighed down by feathers, and walked out.

I breathed in deeply. I slowly let it out and drank the rest of my water. Bright side. Positivity. Positiveness. Light airy thoughts. I sighed.

No more Prep people, or teachers, that brought a smile to my face.

Maybe it wouldn't be so bad after all.

Chapter 9

· · · · · · · · · · ·

I woke up to a dry throat and headache. I groaned. My room was red from the sunlight seeping in; I didn't pay attention to it. I sat up so quickly I hit my head on the cover of my sleeping pod. *Oww.*

I remembered that I would soon be No Longer in Prep. I felt a smile swallow my face. I was too busy being happy to notice my forehead throbbing.

As I stood up I realized two things. 1. Ibis didn't use her Profile. 2. She worked for Teak. That's what had been so weird about Ibis. When she sat next to me, her skin had been right where it showed. She wasn't following any Trends and she had been running.

As I walked into my closet I thought about one of the things I hated most about Profiles. It was that you could still feel the person behind the mask, it was the weirdest feeling. I remember it with my mom. I had run up to grab her hand that was out of reach but I had walked into her. I remember seeing my mom, her stick thin body a couple centimeters in front of me, but I was touching her skin, her Real skin anyway. I felt sick. It then made sense to me why people didn't touch. You never saw parents hug kids, or a teacher pat a student on the back. It just didn't happen. Just like the building.

It made sense that Profile engineers didn't want to mess with our sense of touch, but it might have been a lot less gross if they had. I hated running into people that were supposed to be further away. Seriously, some people are really… substantial. It's gross, because you don't get to see the..substance. It's pretty freaky actually, because it's like you're invisible. They could look like, anything really. I hated it when they were *really* big underneath their Profile, because then they were extra mean when you ran into them. *It's not my problem you just hide behind your mask.*

I reached down to touch my pants and realized why they were made of expandable material.

My pants were soft but stretchy. The material our clothes were made of was very close to an elastic material that they used to use called spandex. It practically molded to your body and was like a second skin. I liked it, I just wish they had designed clothes in different colors or styles.

Fifteen "different" shirts that were all the same got pretty old after a while. I thought of what I could do with my clothes as I put them on, I thought of all the different color combinations that I could use. Why didn't they cut the fabric a different way? It took me *forever* to do and it never looked very good.

———————

I walked to school avoiding the topic the whole way. *Ibis. Who's Ibis? I don't know, so why would I meet her in an old building?* I knew that's where he meant when he said she knew where to find me. Not only was it ominous, it was rude. *And even if I did know her I'm sure we would've met in awkward circumstances, and theoretically, you probably wouldn't even know anything about her. What if she convinces people to walk out a kilometer away from civilization and kills them in old buildings — theoretically?* On the other hand, who knew what Teak would do if I didn't show. He might....*well honestly, what could he do? Send Ibis to kill me?*

As I walked up the school steps I took a deep breath in and slowly let it out. I had time to decide…as long as I didn't get kicked out again. I bit back a smile at the thought. Who would've ever guessed that Jessica Finche would get kicked out of Prep? The very last person on that list was Jessica Finche herself.

I watched as several groups slowly drifted toward me. All waiting to be the first ones to talk to the girl who got kicked out of class. They hadn't even heard that I was *illegally* giving away tablets. After I threw my shoulders back, I made sure to look straight ahead, and put on my very best evil face. I kept on walking even as a few feathered people tried to stand in my way. I did slow down once I saw Savana and Os saunter toward me. I slowed to a stop and my eyes were drawn to her clear claws. Instead of nails, she had opted for pointed talons. She shifted her weight to one hip.

"So, you're *so* much better than us, *surprise, surprise.* The 'my daddy's a senator so I do what I want' mentality has kind of burned out," She pouted her lips, "Which is unfortunate."

"Yeah, don't you hate missed opportunities," I shrugged. She got irritated. I tried not to laugh, it didn't really work.

"Something funny?" She spat.

"Nothing that you would understand," I heard an intake of breath and looked to see we had acquired an audience.

"See, the only reason you think you're better, let alone smarter, is because of your dad." She said with a toss of her beige hair. I wanted to pluck out every fake feather.

"You're giving him *way* too much credit Savana." I looked at her and something on my face must have said enough, because she backed down.

"What are you wearing?" I had never been so grateful to hear Tal's' voice. She strode up, showing of her new horns. Now they weren't just long and curled, they changed color too. I heard mutters going around the entrance. Tal hadn't even looked at me yet. She was too busy showing off her parents' money. And having a Trend-off with Savana. No doubt getting the newest Trend before it came out had cost quite a few credits. I just waited and waited. After several insults had been tossed and Savana retreated, she turned to face me.

"So, what do you think?" Tal smiled and tilted her head, ignoring whatever insult Savana had spat her way.

"They're cool," *They're kind of boring, three colors, that's really the best you can do?* If the Profile engineers could make them change colors from orange to pink why couldn't they make them move? If I were an engineer I would make them curl, or maybe uncurl?

"She's so bent," She laughed and looked over my head at the girl in question.

Then started another day just like the rest. Tal had even forgot about Campaigning. Except, today was going to be different. I had decided. I was going to meet Ibis. I was kind of over the whole "what if she kills me" scenario. Anything would be better than going back to this every day. I was officially over Prep.

Chapter 10

· · · · · · · · · · · ·

Another boring day at school had come and gone, but that was the last day of Jess-from-Prep. I had filled the water bottle Ibis had given me along with my own light blue one. I was ready for Jess-from-Medi. I was okay with it. I was totally ready. I was now making an internal list of things I liked, number 1. I like Medis.

Number 2. I liked water bottles. They had a cooling system inside. They were pretty cool, *Jess, it was only kind of punny, don't get ahead of yourself.* When I was little, mom gave me a tablet on folk tales. There was one with a thief and a genie; which is a big blue guy that's trapped inside a lamp. I substituted myself for a genie and a lamp for a water bottle and —I entertained myself for hours.

The outside layer of my 'lamp' had a rough middle so it was easy to grip and about four different layers until it carried water. The first layer was at the very inside and wasn't porous so that the cooling chemicals in the first two layers in couldn't get through and kill you as you drink. Then the next layer was another protective one, but the third one had this chemical that was always cold, and if someone happened to cut open a water bottle it would burn a hole through their hand. I didn't know if it went through shoes or not, but I wasn't necessarily eager to find out.

Well, I kind of was.... but I didn't really have anything to cut the water bottle with. I was actually more interested in what would happen if I sprayed the yummy-nummy chemicals in someones face. Maybe if Teak was around I could test it out.

I walked past the sagging fence without hesitation, pushed the clear button on the dome control panel, and marched to the building.

Once I was there I slowed until I felt my way to the door in about half the time it had taken me before. It was open.

"Ibis!" I yelled as I walked through. How did she open the door? I had tried so hard but it wouldn't budge. It's not fair. *Seriously, you were just thinking about whether or not she would kill you out here. Now you're jealous of her?* I ignored my conscience. I didn't like feeling guilty or conflicted, or anything negative really.

I wondered if the door slid open. I walked up to it, and looked at it. *Nope,* it was open at an angle. It definitely didn't slide. I had my head stuck through the door when I heard banging coming down from above.

"Hey Jess!" Ibis peered over the edge of the second story floor. Her eyes glimmered and she smiled mischievously.

"How did you?" I gestured wildly to the door.

I looked up and saw her take something from around her neck and throw it down. It fell to the ground with a clang. I shot her an annoyed look. She *could* just use words like a normal human.

I walked over to the thing she had thrown. It was made of plastic.

It was almost like a circle that curved into a short ridge of teeth on one side and was flat on the other. It was hooked onto a rope made of the same material as my clothes. The thing was in the Weird category for sure. I picked it up. It was flat and didn't do anything. *Borrrrinnngggg.* I thought Accel was full of cool gadgets so much for that myth.

I turned it over to the round part. Maybe you had to draw the open sign with it? I walked over to the door and tried it. It didn't work. I tried it over the handle. Nothing moved. Maybe I was doing it wrong? I held the part with the ridges and moved my hands apart and up. OPEN. I heard laughter from above. My face was red.

"Just tell me," I turned around.

Ibis snickered. *I'm going to throw this stupid thing at you.*

"Try it in the keyhole Jess," She suggested with a smile. *Why don't you stick your face in the keyhole?*

I huffed and turned back around and looked for a "keyhole," whatever that was. I searched and saw nothing. My eyes kept on coming back to the handle, where in the middle there was what I had always assumed was a crack. Now that I looked closely, it was too wide and symmetrical to be a crack.I stuck the thing in it and turned. Something clicked. I smiled. *HA, did it! Take that.*

"Where did you get it?" I asked as I walked toward Ibis.

"I made it actually," a deeper voice—definitely *not* Ibis, answered. *They're going to kill you. Run and hide. That's why Teak told you to meet here, she works for Teak and she's going to kill you because he's angry with what you did.*

I slowly looked up, and I saw the owner of the voice on the second floor, next to Ibis.

He had ruffled hair and dark skin. Darker than most, since the Trend was pale. He had a pretty decent looking Profile, but I wondered what made him decide to keep the larger than socially-acceptable nose.

I felt my face heat up as I saw him stare back at me with out-of-date blue eyes. Normally people looked me over then moved on, but he hadn't. That meant that I had been standing here, looking him over, not saying anything, just staring at him in silence. *Nice one Jess. Checkin' out your killer.* I turned redder.

"How?" I cleared my throat and tried to draw attention away from myself. It worked. His face lit up. "It took me a while to figure it out actually. For the first few months we had to get in with the garage door, but it killed me that we couldn't use the front door. You know?" He looked at me earnestly.

I quickly grunted. I *grunted*.

Yeah, that's real cute Jess, do it again. Then I winced after I realized what it had sounded like. He gave me a concerned look then went on.

"Yeah, so I went back to HQ and I told Cas, 'hey, can you hook me up with some putty?'" I nodded like this was an everyday conversation about tails. *What's putty?*

"So she did, and I took it here and shoved it inside the keyhole which didn't really work that well, but it turned out half decent. Then I took a scan of it then printed it out and boom!" He pointed to the key in my hand. "There you have it." He smiled at the end, "So technically I beat the door."

Ibis huffed. "Roman, you can't beat things that aren't alive."

"It's very rude," I added on smiling. *Ohh, nice one Jess, you're getting it, slowly but surely.*

"Umm hello, old *old* saying, but correct me if I'm wrong; Don't beat a dead horse." Roman stated pointedly. Before Ibis could cut in to contradict him, he was off again.

"It's not like I just left it at that though," he quickly reassured me. "Then I made this little scanner that takes dimensions and everything and then prints them out, then I made myself a nicer key." Ibis stared him down. "But, you have the original," he defended himself.

I covered a smile I hadn't realized was on my face while I was listening to them argue. They were fine with being relaxed and laid back.

Not like Prep, every thought that crossed their empty brains was the most important thing they could possibly think of. Ibis and —Roman, could talk about it.

Tal would've loved Roman, except for the fact that he talked back. I looked at him closer and saw there was a bright reflection of something small and shiny behind his ear. *Weird.*

"So, Iby here tells me that we're supposed to bring you with us?" Roman's sentence got more unsure with each word. My eyes darted away from the small piece on his neck. I was determined to figure out what it was, and to do that, I would have to get closer.

"Well, see, here's the thing. Teak's mad at me because I…didn't *not* give old tablets to Medis which, isn't even something to be punished for, but now….he's making me switch Tracks. I'm going to be in Medi. " I swallowed.

"I didn't not," He mouthed smiling. When he smiled, the corner of his mouth crinkled, which pushed his ears back in an almost endearing way. It stopped being endearing when it suddenly

moved the chip out of my sight.

Ibis looked at him with irritation written all over her face. He

was making friends and she didn't like it. I tried not to laugh.

"So you don't *really* have to bring me with you, do you?" I

asked nonchalantly.

"Yeah, we do." Ibis looked at Roman sternly.

"But, I'm really sorry that you have to leave your Track, but

you'll be better off. I promise," Ibis tried to look sympathetic.

I looked at Roman. He just grinned and I noticed he had an

indent on his right cheek when he smiled. *What a dirt sack.* So much

for friends.

"Now?" I asked nervously. *We are currently leaving my life as I*

know it. I'm joining Medi. Which is totally fine, nervousness is

synonymous with excitement. So we're all set.

Ibis and Roman raced down the steps, hands skimming a rickety metal rail that I hadn't even noticed.

"Well, come on!" She grabbed my arm as I roughly pulled it out her grasp. She quickly dropped my arm.

"Sorry, I forgot, no touchy." She shrugged apologetically.

Roman walked over and gently tapped my shoulder with his index finger which was oddly cold. I quickly pulled away and took a couple steps back, until I backed up into a wall that rasped my back. *What is wrong with these people?* I tensed my jaw. *It's ok. They're in Accel, they're weird, bumping into people and touching them is normal.*

"That's interesting." Roman muttered, looking me over. I glared at him, pretending his words didn't make the hairs on my neck stand up, but he didn't seem to notice.

"Leave her alone, Ro," She said softly. *Ro, of course she gave him a cute nickname.*

"Alright, sorry about that, come on, I promise I won't touch you again, let's just go, we're late." Ibis motioned me forward. And being the clueless person I was, I followed.

Chapter 11

. . . .

I felt I had been walking for what seemed like ages, and I had only found empty classrooms. I was tempted to open the message that had been blinking in my wrist since I was at the building, ignored it and kept walking. Ibis had just left me at the entrance of a looming white building in the Accel district, with no directions to give me except for a name. Roman had gone before I had even noticed his absence. I was about to give up when I heard noise from around the corner. I walked into a room with lights hanging from the ceiling and the air was wet and heavy.

I looked straight ahead and saw spiraling white towers that were filled with what looked like dirt and leafy—things, that must have been projected.

I walked over past all the people who had suddenly stopped talking. *Whatever, I'm not going to see any of you ever again after today.* I told myself to ignore the stares as I kneeled down at the base of a spiral and poked the dirt that was in between the rungs separating the foliage. It felt moist beneath my finger. I felt a tug of embarrassment after I imagined what I looked like, but I pushed it away. I scooped the brown material up in my hand and was surprised to feel that it was rough and …squishy, but in a nice way. I smiled. I reached over and tried to swipe my hand through the green floppy projection, and ending up hitting the definitely-real plant and ripping off a round green bud.

"You can't just walk in here and start smacking my legumes." A short blond boy with freckles said, getting frustrated.

"Is that what this is?" I tried to ignore his whiny attitude. I liked dirt. And the plant stuff. Not him.

"Actually," A wiry girl cast a withering glare his way, "Those are tomatoes"

"So what's the green part?" I gestured. The girl then redirected her stare to me. I raised my eyebrows and squared my shoulders. She looked away angrily and I smirked. My staring contests was interrupted by a scratchy high pitched voice.

"Um, yeah, hi, my name is Argi, cool nice to meet you too. Sure you can touch my dirt and my peppers, thanks for asking. But what are you doing here?" The short kid tried to look anywhere but my face while he asked.

"Looking for Dale—I think that's his name, which ones are peppers?" I looked at him, as he shakily pointed to one of the higher plants that I hadn't even touched.

"And, don't worry I'm only here for the day" I smiled sweetly.

"So there's this great thing called nature, and nature grows food, then we pick that food, then we eat it." He looked at me carefully. I nodded slowly, ok so he was passive aggressive, and was trying to show his dominance in a really pathetic attempt at mockery. *I don't have to see you ever again.*

"So is that your job, Argi? *Do you eat food?* Is that your thing?" Every time he opened his mouth to answer I added another question, *take that.*

The wiry girl who had glared at him earlier spoke up, "Lay off."

I laughed, "You first."

I turned so I could look at both of them, "What a let down, I always thought Accels were the best and brightest, but I can honestly say the best part about you and your track so far, has been the plants."

The wiry girl dropped all emotion from her face. Except for the curl of her lip, "So we rocked the first impressions, huh?"

I looked around and found a black tube that was dripping water to all the plants. I looked up to the bright lamps that hurt my eyes. And those lights must be instead of sunlight.

"You don't eat tofu?" I asked as I turned around. My hand felt grimy and dirty so I wiped it on my pants.

"Not really, the fresher stuff tastes way better," *Obviously.* The wiry girl paced when she spoke.

"So how come everyone else has to eat it?"

No one answered. "I get it, only the best get the best, it's been a solid totalitarian philosophy, I'd stick with it," I shrugged as I thought about it. I saw the girl stop pacing.

I just wish someone had offered *me* peppers, but then again I wasn't *the best.* "Well I guess it's better that way," I said quietly in thought.

"Are you Dale's?" A collection of murmurs and nodding went around the Accel kids.

"I guess," I said annoyed. I wanted a pepper, at least a tomato. I didn't care if I wasn't good enough.

"There you are," A familiar voice asked from the doorway. No one was offering me a pepper. I was getting frustrated, I didn't even glance at Ibis leaning on the door. Was I really going to have to ask for it? I suddenly felt a tug on my arm.

I snapped my head around to Ibis to glare at her.

"I'll get you one later, ok?" She said knowingly. I rolled my eyes and looked away.

———

Dale ended up being a lady. A very tall lady, I could tell even though she was sitting down. I swallowed nervously. This was the person I was meeting instead of Teak. I had no idea why. An image of a lone pepper floated through my head. *Focus.*

She was petting a four legged animal that I had never heard of before. It had a round small head and a wide large shell on its back, and it was eating a pair of pants. *It probably eats people too.*

I looked back up at Dale who just stared down at me with big blue eyes.

"Sooo, number one you broke a rule." Her eyes widened as she spoke.

"Yeah, hi," *What is she talking about? Ohh, my tablets.*

"So, why?" She threw her hands up, the monster paused its pants eating and gave her an exasperated look, then she resumed petting it.

"Well, it was for a friend and I had finished reading them—"

"Your score"—she pulled out a tablet, "Was on the upper cusp of average. If you hadn't taken your time, do you know what would've happened?" She asked bluntly. She waited for an answer.

"What, I thought I was here because of the tablets and —" *To change to Medi, that's why Teak came to my house and threatened me. Right? And how did you know —*

"You would be here, that's what you'd be." She smiled and blinked like that was great news. *Well, now I'm really glad I stuck with Tal.*

"But I'm not, here, and I'm getting kicked out of Prep and sent to Medi" I said as my eyes scanned the room that was filled with chairs, but no tables, and more animals like the one on the ground. *At least I'm not going to be in Accel.*

"Plus, how did you know that I slowed down my time on the test?" I crossed my arms over my chest. Teak had *so* many reasons to kick me out of Prep.

"You know those little scanners for the cubes," She widened her eyes and frowned as she shot her head out, hair flying.

"Well, yeah, you—"

"Those are cameras." She smiled, sat back and let it sink in.

"Sooo…." I tried not to sound as exasperated as her pet looked.

"Sooo, we could hear everything you were saying. I mean no one watches those videos, but when Teak told me you were switching Tracks, I pulled it up. What I saw was a little surprising." She crossed her arms, and raised her eyebrows expectantly.

I winced and shifted in my seat. I remembered my chant. *Do what a Prep would do.* Classic Jess. Dale widened her eyes and tilted her head forward. I felt a tick in my jaw.

"Well, I wanted to be with my friend, so I, just did what I could to stay with her. It was stupid, but I couldn't change it." I was already tired of this conversation.

"Yeah, well then fix it, and go make it better," she smiled and shook her head at me. *Oh yeah, sure, let me get on that.* I thought about it for a second.

I stopped. Dale had said something that rang a bell.

"Go" she shooed me, "Go, Teak's been waiting for you for a while, next door." I gave her my best annoyed look. *Can I just go back to Prep, please? I'll never be nice or helpful again, I promise.*

I backed away from Dale and quickly walked out the sliding plastic door and to the left. In the next room sat an impatient President. I swallowed and sat down in a hard plastic chair. He now had thin black spikes covering his skin, like feathers on a bird. His eyes were thin slits that reflected when you looked directly at them, I averted my eyes.

"Sorry Teak, that…director didn't tell me you were here until, well, just now really, and—"

"Do you want to be in Prep *now*, Jessica?" He asked, his face calm, not a spike was stirring. *Uh oh.* I sucked in a breath. I looked down and caught a glimpse of his hands laying on the milk whit desk; gently clasped, and where there should have been nails, on each finger, there was a single feather.

"Yes, I'm *really* sorry, I won't do it again just please don't make me leave, I—" He nodded pointedly.

"See, we never appreciate what we have until it's gone, isn't that true?" I sighed in relief. He had to know how hard I worked to be in the top 10.

"Yes, you're right, and I realize it, and I really want to stay in Prep," I said, trying to make eye contact with his diamond shaped pupils.

He tsked and his eyelids blinked separately. "Well that's unfortunate, really, you had your chance. You didn't view it as an opportunity, so, from now on you're in—" I didn't hear the rest.

I was imagining what it would be like to be in Medi, I would have to have children, have to go to work everyday, and I would have to talk to people and pretend that I enjoyed their company, unlike Prep, people would want you to engage in conversation. I had convinced myself that I would be ok with it. All I had done was prove that I was either gullible or a superb lier. I felt sick.

"But first, you have to re-test," He said offhandedly as he scratched his arm with a flexible nail. I looked at him. His feather hair rustled without a breeze. How could he have been so blasé about this?

I numbly pushed out of my uncomfortable chair and walked over to where he pointed, at two different testing areas. I silently sat down in the chair. The clear round wall closed around me and I started the test.

They had the same blocks with the same designs that I had to make years ago. I couldn't even bring myself to fake smile as my favorite block patterns portion of the test came around. After the pointless math questions, came the very last question. The question that I had given the wrong answer to before.

"JESSICA FINCHE," the voice said, "If something is broken, what do you do? A: Fix it, B: Leave it, or C: Make something better. You have thirty seconds."

I smiled grimly. I remembered what Dale had said., *28*. There wasn't really a choice, I was going to end up in Medi anyway, *24*. So why not just answer it truthfully? *20,* It wasn't like it was going to change anything. *18* "C, make something better."

I sighed after the clear doors opened. It was over, I got out of my chair but I turned around to see that on the screen it said in bright green letters; CONGRATULATIONS.

What? Are you kidding me. I stood up and shoved the chair away. I glared at the stupid screen and thought about throwing the pointless cubes. I walked out the doors to where Teak had been sitting.

He was gone.

Chapter 12

. . . .

The problem with belonging is that you have to have something to belong to.

My first problem, was that when I got up to ask Teak what was going on, he was nowhere to be found.

My second problem was that I didn't know which Track I was in.

"Teak!" I yelled. *Where is he?* I felt bad after yelling. It was a good thing they didn't hear me or else they probably would have another excuse to kick me out. *As if they needed any more.* I looked out the doorway I had come in through, and down both ways of the hall. I kept walking.

You could tell you were in Accel just from looking at the building. There were bright colors everywhere, along with tiny tablets perched on the walls that projected little holograms of what was going on in all the different rooms.

I walked closer to the holograms and saw Dale's tall frame talking to a few Accel kids. The problem was that I had no idea how to get to her. I sighed and turned my head left and right. I quickly decided on turning right and I quickly walked through the halls.

It wasn't that quickly, since I stopped and looked at all the classrooms. There were several with shelves full of tablets and others filled with machinery. Then there was a whole hallway dedicated entirely to Printers. I had never seen a real Printer before. All that anyone in Accel had to do was send their design to the Printer along with material specifications and they had whatever they needed. It's how Roman made his key.

I walked on. I was about to give up when I saw Ibis on one of the holograms.

She was walking out of the door just as she saw me.

Ibis smiled. "So, what did you get?" She asked excitedly.

I didn't really have time for her. "Where's Teak?"

She firmly planted her feet in the ground, "What did you get?"

"I got 'Congratulations' at the end of the test, ok, but it doesn't matter since I'm going to Medi. Where's Teak, I don't really know what to do now." I said quickly as I scanned behind Ibis to make sure he wasn't hiding.

Ibis sighed. "You're no fun, you know that?" She put a hand on her hip.

"I never said I was," I turned around to look behind me. "Where is he?" I muttered.

Ibis sighed and looked down at her hands.

"I'm going to give you a tour, ok?"

"I'd rather not, *thank you*," I glared at her.

"It's not an option," She snapped back.

She grabbed my arm and walked me down the hallway explaining the entire way. I focused on her short hair slightly swaying when she walked.

"This is the Ops board." She pointed up at a screen that had different rows filled with numbers that were switching —the number of people needed to complete it, and very broad descriptions—like "malfunction." It looked exactly like Prep Leaderboards, except these ones were real.

"Medis have Fixings, but here we call them Operations, or Ops," She pulled me along, "There will be all sorts of problems, but for the ones that happen two or more times, Medis send us that information and what's happening, then we find a solution, and make something to fix it permanently, then make it better than before." I was looking at all the different people in Accel, I felt overwhelmed.

"Then we have the Profiles department, all the coders are there, umm, then we have Inventions and Innovations, which is where you—" I looked into the room that Ibis was chatting about, it had different gears and a whole wall filled with different types of ropes and another filled entirely with different materials.

Ibis grinned, "I thought you might like this one, Teak told me about your flashlight, and the thing you do with tablets." I walked inside the room and looked at all the different types of cords, wires, gears, you name it.

I stopped when Ibis tugged on my arm. I looked at her sternly, "Ibis, where is he?"

She sighed, "I can't—I want to tell you, but the director should explain it to you."

I was impatient, "Ibis, I already met Dale, the one with that pants-eating-thing"

She laughed, "It's a tortoise, and Dale's not the director, the director was busy, so I sent you to meet Dale instead." Her eyes glazed over. Like my moms' did when she used her Profile. I didn't know Ibis used a Profile. I tried to swipe my hand above her arm, but I didn't hit her Real skin. I frowned and tapped her wrist, definitely Real. Weird. Ibis suddenly came out of her daze.

"Actually, the director is ready to see you now," She pulled me away from the room and quickly marched me across the hall. She opened the door and I saw a short lady with straight blond hair and green eyes. She looked oddly familiar. I sat down in the plush orange chair that was in the middle of the room.

The woman's eyes twinkled. "Hi Jess," She looked like she was trying to bite back a laugh. "You don't recognize me?" I was *so* over Accel people.

"No, I don't, and before you disclose this obviously very obvious fact, can you please call Teak in, or tell me where he is because I'm switching to Medi, my career is over before it's even begun, and I don't really know what to do." I summarized. I leaned back deeper into my orange chair.

I hadn't noticed her eyes glazed over until I finished talking. *Thanks for listening.* I heard a knock on the door. I let out a breath through my nose, *seriously?*

A heavy set man walked through the door. I glared at him until he sat down uncomfortably in another orange chair next to mine. Who was he? He tried to inconspicuously move his chair further away from mine by messing with the settings on the arm rest, it didn't work since we were both watching him.

"Thank you for coming, Teak," She said sardonically. What? *I guess this is Teak sans Profile*. He was ugly. No wonder he used a Profile. And without it, he looked empty. Pasty and hollow, and sad. *And totally defeat-able.*

He looked at me uncomfortably, "Hello Miss Finche, I hope you are excited for your transition to—"

The blond lady cleared her throat delicately, "Well, I was just going to tell Jessica why she was in *Accel*, but maybe you can explain to her what your job is."

"What." I seethed at the green eyed woman.

"I'm not in Accel. I was in Prep, then Medi. Then your test told me I was in the 'Congratulations' track, which is very thoughtful and heartfelt I'm sure, but see the funny thing is, that at this point, where I am right now," I smiled viscously, "Is not a point for congratulating me on getting into an unidentified track. So, It would be much appreciated if we could get to the *actual* track

I'm in since there seems to be a lot of confusion around that issue."

I glared at Teak, who looked slightly bored with my rant. I didn't bother looking at the woman since I could tell she was smiling. I intensified my glare.

Teak sighed heavily then turned slightly to face me. "My job is to find people who don't belong,"

"Not what I asked—"I tried to cut in.

"I find them in Tracks where they don't belong, then I help them choose a new Track, the one they belong in," Teak went on. "And I have a very small division of people who help me. Your father used to be one of them." I looked down at my hands then after I realized I had broken eye contact, I made sure to keep emotions off my face.

He said that I hadn't belonged in Prep. I hadn't realized how worried I was about not belonging, well, anywhere. I belonged in Medi. *I knew it.* I was also kind of disappointed.

"I am sorry that I had to be…tough on you, it's just that at the time, your father was trying to push the issue that Medis shouldn't be payed as much, which is—anyway, you were doing *all* the wrong things at *all* the wrong times. He didn't know that you were the one giving that family tablets, he had just heard about it, and that gave him even more reason to be angry; 'Medis shouldn't be buying tablets,' He said." Teak was getting on my nerves.

There was *no way* my dad could've said that, he wasn't the nicest guy, but, saying Medis were overpaid? That was low, even for him.

"So, your mother gave me the tip a few years back, but in all honesty I didn't believe her, until she insisted and I looked at your testing videos." He shifted in his seat. *My mom did what?* When did she have enough time for that? "I had to be sure, so you've been on watch for a few years now—"

"Excuse me, but what do you mean I've been 'watched' for a few years?" I snapped at him.

"Well, we had to make sure—"

"And it took you, *years*?" I smiled and nodded my head, I started using the baby voice—the one that I used when I talked to Preps I didn't like, "Honestly, it only takes a week to look at someone and say, 'Hey, you know, they look pretty, actually, *extraordinarily*, miserable, more so than usual, maybe, I don't know, maybe there's a reason, like they've been in the wrong Track for seven years.' You know, your programs are pretty weak if they can't detect an ordinary nine year-old lying." I screwed my mouth at the ends and shrugged in a what-can-ya-do kind of way. Teaks hollow face got red.

"Well, uh, two things actually, one. You weren't an average nine year old that's why—"

"You're just full of contradictions Teak, you know that?"
His hands gripped his knees. His jaw ticked.

"Well you're in Accel now, so what does it matter? You're ungrateful," He spat.

I was too busy glaring at him to process what he had said.

"That's enough!" The blond woman had lost her smile.

"I was going to ask if you wanted to work in my division—" Teak ignored her.

"She didn't know she was in Accel yet," She sent a frosty glare in his direction. He swallowed then turned in his chair.

"You belong in Accel Jessica, " He amended, "Obviously." I looked at his pale skin and lackluster chestnut hair.

I tried to be deadpan. "I'm in Accel?" No thanks.

The blond lady smiled. Teak grimaced.

Both their eyes glazed over. *It was just getting exciting.*

"It looks like you have an Ops too," Teak said dryly.

"You're kidding me, right?" I looked at him, "I *just found* out I'm in Accel,"

"Jess, you should be excited, it's what you've always wanted," I snapped my head around to look at the blond lady. Only one other person said my name like that, made the "ess" last noticeably longer than it should. She wasn't that tall, and she had a round nose, curly hair, and grey eyes, not green. I searched her face and I realized who she was.

Teak stood up with difficulty and motioned me toward the door, "Come on, you'll be late, again!"

I tried to stand in the doorway and look at the woman, I could only give a confused glance to her small wave before I left. *Bye mom.*

Chapter 13

. . . .

I wasn't wearing pants.

At least it didn't feel like it. When everyone had their backs turned I bent my knees and lunged to the sides, these pants were thin. Unlike normal pants, they didn't stick to your skin, they were loose until they tightened at mid-calf, it felt like they weren't there. I had to stop lunging and pretend I had dropped something after I made eye contact with an Accel.

Teak had sent for Ibis to come and grab me, we were partners, or in a team, or something. I actually had no idea what was going on. I had been shuttled out of Accel and thrust onto this flat dock that connected to the back of the building, we had stood on a white dock with safety rails that dropped slowly until we hit an area below ground. I didn't like it, and I told Ibis, she had just punched my arm.

Ibis, the person in question, turned around and gave me a lopsided grin, "So this is just a regular Ops, it's with a turbine, so once we get there we'll meet up with the group of Medis, they'll explain what's wrong and what's causing the problem. But, Teak tells me you'll be in our division, So that means usually we'll be working mostly with people." She motioned me forward as I heard the quiet thud and metal whirring of machinery bring the thick platform we had stood on a second ago back to where it had come from. I watched the dock slowly rise, but my gaze was pulled away as I looked up in awe at the rough ceiling of a tunnel that was carved out of the earth.

I nodded absently. *I'm in Accel now. I wear not-pants, and I invent things, we talk to Medis, and do stuff in tunnels, and it's legal.* It didn't sound right.

She looked at me, "You're where you belong now Jess," I forced the corners of my mouth up, "Then we'll figure out a way to fix what your dad's doing," I dropped my smile.

"What's he doing, apart from amazing parenting?"

Ibis looked like she just about done with being my designated babysitter, "Teak didn't tell you?" I shook my head.

She leaned in and whispered,"Jess, he's trying to make Medis work for free," Well, I knew he was bad, and that was bad, but it wasn't the *worst* thing that he could've done. When he got irritated I had asked him for a tablet as a present, he told me grandma had died, on my birthday.

"Do you remember those people in the old days called slaves?" I nodded my head, "He's running a campaign to make them like *slaves*, Jess," She searched my eyes. I didn't give her anything to go on.

"But you can help us, you can make him see that he's wrong." She said it with enthusiasm, but I could tell she expected it to be resolved easily. She didn't know that he was *very* far from being amicable, let alone easily persuaded.

"I don't think it's going to be that easy," Her face hardened. I had never seen Ibis look anything less than friendly, and I took an imperceptible step back. *So this is why I'm in Accel.* It suddenly made sense. Ibis could tell the conversation was over.

"Come on, we're heading out, you don't get seasick do you?" Ibis asked over her shoulder.

"What's seasick?" She laughed and pulled me into a silver tube-like capsule. I followed and just as the clear door started closing, someone sprinted through just as it shut and the bottom of their shirt got caught in the door. The person pulled their shirt so hard it ripped out of the closed doors, and fell on me. The assaulter ended up being Roman. Of course.

Chapter 14

. . . .

Roman suddenly turned around, his face centimeters from mine. I focused on holding my breath and turning my face away from his curled lips. I tried not to notice how his darker skin contrasted strongly against the whites of his eyes. I was so focused on looking anywhere but his face that I hadn't realized the silver capsule had submerged into the ocean, barely squeaking on thick white rails that were built on the ocean floor inside tight clear tubes. I backed away from Roman and walked around the capsule which could hold around 20 people. I tried to focus on the fact that we just went *under* the dome. My mind obviously couldn't handle being in awe, so I shifted my attention to the Transport.

There were only 6 or 7 occupants. I concentrated on listing my surroundings, but I couldn't keep his eyes off my mind. I looked up and saw the top of the transport had just gone under water. All that was visible through the clear doors was the green murky ocean we had been pulled under. I touched the door which felt cool under my fingers. I rested my palm on it until the transport jerked roughly.

The transport hissed in surprise at being deprived of air, and the noise intensified as we picked up speed and plunged straight down. I lost my footing and grabbed desperately at the nearest handle. I looked around and realized why some of the Accels were attached to the transport walls by straps. with another slight jerk, I threw my arm out to a smooth grey strap and held on. I held it appreciatively. *Not white. I could get used to this*. As we sped up, the transport was surrounded with bubbles, it mirrored popping in my ears that started out slowly but soon escalated to rapid, painful bursts. Without warning, I felt something wet running down my face, as I looked at my reflection in the closed doors flashing white from the bars of the tunnel the transport was in, I saw streams of red streaking down my face and could taste something metallic on my tongue.

I pushed my hands up to my nose, and the pain got even worse, it felt like someone was closing my head in a door and my brain was being squeezed out my ears. I let out a scream and sank to my knees. I looked up and saw Romans blurry face in front of mine.

I could barely make out what he was saying, "Forgot, Ibis —the pills." He frantically grabbed something from Ibis and tried to push my hands away from my nose. Somehow he managed to shove two tiny spheres in my mouth and then started yelling.

"Swallow them, Jess!" I shook my head violently, it would hurt worse. I felt a stab of pain pulse sharply in my head.

"We need you, come on, please, just, do it!" I felt the pills try to stick to my tongue as I swallowed them.

I held in another scream as another tidal wave of pain rocked my head. Then, the pressure was swept away.

My nose was still bleeding, but Roman took out a small white device shaped like a U. He quickly fitted it to the bridge of my nose until it started heating up and I pushed him away. The white U was burning my skin and I pulled it off and threw it at him.

"Get away," My voice was hoarse. I saw a flicker of something register in Romans' eyes. I didn't dwell on it. I started coughing and Ibis walked over with a water bottle. I only had enough energy to glare.

"Sorry about that, I totally forgot about the pressure pills for when we go under. Sinking to the ocean floor can do that to a person." I didn't look at her.

She crouched down in front of me and held out the water bottle.

"This seems familiar doesn't it?" I coughed at her in response.

"Here," She laughed and handed me the bottle which I hastily drank. She got up and walked over to the side with handles on the ceiling. I took the bottle and threw it at her back. I somehow managed to aim, and it bounced off her shoulder. She spun around and looked at me.

"You'll do just fine here." I groaned and looked for something else to throw. She looked over to the other group of people who I hadn't noticed before. They stood uncertainly, holding fabrics and sprays. I took a long look at them and sighed. I slowly stood up, my vision was wobbly for a moment, but after I stood still, it went away.

I walked over to the person holding the fabric sheets and grabbed one roughly from their hands. Then I snatched another water bottle from a shorter Accel and drenched the soft white fabric and wiped my face until it was raw and the cloth was streaked pink. I looked down at it and balled it up and threw it at Ibis who caught it in one hand. I smirked.

"Welcome to your new home," She bowed, "And you know, experiences make lasting friendships." Her eyes twinkled.

"We'll see," I walked closer and noticed the gentle swaying of the transport. I grabbed a handle just like Ibis had.

"So I'm here, for good?" The capsule rocked gently.

"Unless you really mess something up," She smiled.

"I was going to run for President."

"Things change." Harsh.

"So, about my mom—"

"Are we doing introductions now?" Ibis yelled at the others. My eyes darted to Roman, who was grabbing more water bottles. As they walked over, I started to remember seeing a few of them in the gardening room.

"I'm Caro, the programmer," The wiry girl from the room said. I winced at her tone, "Sorry about before, I was—"

She rolled her eyes, "It's fine, we all get a little nervous before our first Ops." *Right, Even if I didn't know about it.*

A girl with spiky blue hair spoke up "I'm Cas, your defacto coder." She pulled something small and silver out of her pocket.

Cas cut in, "And no, programming *isn't* the same as coding." I nodded.

"Ward, um, remodeling I guess, " was the name of a bulky blond boy. He was almost as big as Q.

Ibis nudged someone who let out a huff and murmured something so quietly I didn't hear it. When I saw who it was, I grinned.

"Hi Argi." I said with my eyebrows raised. He muttered under his breath. I smiled and turned. Right into Roman, who lifted the corner of his mouth and offered me a water bottle. When I reached out to grab it the transport surfaced. The doors opened with a hiss as I quickly took it from his hand. When I we walked out of the transport and onto the slick black dock, the group circled around Ibis.

"We're going to go meet a group of Medis and work on that new design we had for the turbines," Ibis turned to Cas, "You sure you've got the plans?"

Cas glanced at her, "I said I did." She turned to me, "Be nice to them, it'll be weird for you, but they're all just people." I tried not to get irritated with Ibis. We pulled out the six bags that were on the side of the transport and hooked them over our shoulders. I followed their lead and pulled an Oxy-Pack out of my bag.

We started walking to another transport like the one we had just exited, but this time it was above ground. I ignored the feeling of relief surfacing in my chest.

I felt a hand on my shoulder and turned around to see the same dark eyes that had tried to help me earlier.

"Hey."

"Hey," I raised an eyebrow.

"Your nose is only half cauterized." He pulled the straps on his pack snugly on his shoulder. I noticed that when he had something in his hands, he would always move it around. It was almost cute.

"I thought you should know," He nodded and turned to catch up with the group. I watched him as he turned back around.

"Listen, okay, I'm really, *really* sorry about that, in the transport," He ran a hand through his hair, "I got really freaked out, and I just shoved pills in your mouth, and I burnt your nose, but I was only trying to help." Roman was dripping with sincerity. But he could squirm, just a little.

"This has been an awful first day," I admitted, making sure to keep my face blank. He searched my face. A smile quickly appeared and was paired with a throaty laugh. I rolled my eyes and he took two quick steps forward and gently wrapped his arms around me. I felt warmth gushing up inside of me. Roman retracted those steps before I could hug him back.

"So sorry, forgot the personal bubble, won't happen. Ever again. Promise." I didn't say anything against it. A Prep would't want to be hugged. Or ex-Prep anyway.

I walked with him to the transport, sucking on the synthetic oxygen, and had just set down my pack when Cas stood, barring my way. She took the silver object I had seen her holding before and held it in her hand. Before I could ask what it was she had held it up to my face and started talking.

"This, is a microchip,"

"Why do I need another one? I've already got one back here," I tapped the base of my skull where my chip was. Cas looked disgusted.

"You are not buying things, or giving yourself feather eyes, or sending little secret messages to your *bestie*," She curled her lip.

"This is strictly for communicating during Ops." I kept quiet and looked to see a reflection of silver shine from behind her ear.

She held it up closer and I could see microscopic threads running through the chip. Before she opened her mouth, I grabbed it and started asking questions.

"So, how do you transmit feeds? You don't have antennas, so it can't be wavelength." The irritation climbed back on Cas' face.

"We are the antennas, well actually, these," She flicked the back of my neck, "are our antennas, and it is transmitted by radio." I nodded and flipped it over, there was a tiny point in the middle.

"Isn't this a bit twenty-first century?" I motioned at the chip. Cas looked bent.

"Are we still jabbing ourselves with metal to make ourselves unique and pretty?" Ibis punched me and I lost my breath. I looked at Cas and had the dignity to feel embarrassed.

"Sorry Cas, I just tear cool things apart, it's my thing." I shrugged and forced eye contact. I watched the irritation leave her eyes and get replaced with slight satisfaction. *Uh oh.*

"We'll be even in a second," she rummaged around in her deep front pockets which were stained grey from all the use. She pulled out a silver disc as wide around as my thumb. First she held it up near my implanted chip and held it still until it activated with a blue light. Then she took the chip, flipped it and positioned it slightly behind the middle of my ear. I sighed and pulled my stringy hair to the right. She pinched my skin roughly and I tried my best not to wince. She pushed the disk up to my skin as she pushed the middle that resulted in a swift compression that squeezed the sharp end through my skin. I felt my eyes stinging and I kept them closed. I opened them looked at Cas, she was busy putting away the disk. She looked at me and nodded her blue hair.

I had been approved.

The transport stopped with a swing and we walked out the sliding doors to a blistering heat. Above were tall looming poles with propellers flying at the top. I tried to focus on feeling the full Accel effect, I couldn't, and not just because hair being whipped in my mouth was ruining my attempted revelation. I had one last shred of Prep hanging on.I finally looked down at the blinking light in my wrist I had ignored before. On the purple haze was a shiny new message from Tal.

I opened it to see three words; "Change. You're change."

Acknowledgements

· · · · · · · · · · · · · · · · · ·

I'd like to thank my family so much for supporting me while I wrote this book, and for listening to my sing the lion king song after I finished it. It took me about double the time I thought it would, but hey, it's finished(the book, not the song)! I'd like to thank my mom for always being present and willing to brainstorm ideas or being able to help me with "what should happen next." She was the first person to read it, and gave me handwritten notes on each chapter while consulting and running a company, she's always there, cheering me on and encouraging me to improve. Very different from Reyna Finche! Maya, you've been the best sister ever, to quote 90% of souvenir t-shirts(the best sister part, they'll never sell 'Maya' spelled your way). My sister, has throughout the whole process also been (grudgingly) supportive, reading when asked which always ended up being accompanied by "this doesn't make sense." Thank you for that, honestly, critical feedback is appreciated. You've been willing to sit through my interrogations, "What should Jess do?" your answers were usually much more accurate than mine would be, since Jess was based off of you. Don't ever forget that you're the best person you'll ever be! P. Dillard, who has been my writing inspiration. You've just been the best friend I could ask for. You're always so supportive and you always push me to be better, and you always go above and beyond, so thanks. Along with all my editors; my english teacher, Mr. Slater, who is an actual author, took the time to read my book and give feedback, thanks so much. Along with the countless other people who have taken the time out of their busy lives to read LTM, I can't thank you enough! Oh and John and Hank Green, Vlogbrothers really got me excited about being nerd-fighterly cool, and helped me think, "Hey, maybe I should write some of this down." Actually no, sorry John and Hank, the writing it down part goes to my mom, but you did help by providing thought provoking literature and funny videos. That helped.

About the Author

. . . .

Irk is a first-time author as well as publisher. Irk lives in Nevada, with a loving family. Irk spends time running cross-country, playing lacrosse, designing graphics, and reading, but mostly editing. Lots and lots of editing. Irk has tried and failed at many things, but believes that once you focus, and visualize results, they'll come one way or another.

22853628R00115

Made in the USA
Middletown, DE
11 August 2015